REALITY
SQUALL

Reality Squall

J. KRAWCZYK

N*P

NOSETOUCH PRESS

CHICAGO | PITTSBURGH

REALITY SQUALL

© 2024 by Jason Krawczyk
All Rights Reserved.

ISBN-13: 978-1-944286-41-5
Paperback Edition

Published by Nosetouch Press
www.nosetouchpress.com

For more information, contact Nosetouch Press:
info@nosetouchpress.com

This book is a work of fiction. Names, characters, places,
and incidents either are products of the authors imaginations
or are used fictitiously. Any resemblance to actual persons,
living or dead, events, or locales is entirely coincidental.

Cataloging-in-Publication Data

Names: Krawczyk, Jason, author.
Title: Reality Squall
Description: Chicago, IL : Nosetouch Press [2024]
Identifiers: ISBN: 9781944286415 (paperback)
Subjects: LCSH: Psychological fiction—Fiction. |
Speculative fiction—Fiction. |
GSAFD: Surrealist fiction. | Psychological fiction.
BISAC: FICTION / Psychological.

Cover & Interior Designed by Christine M. Scott
www.clevercrow.com

FOR MOM, MOMS, DAD AND DADS.

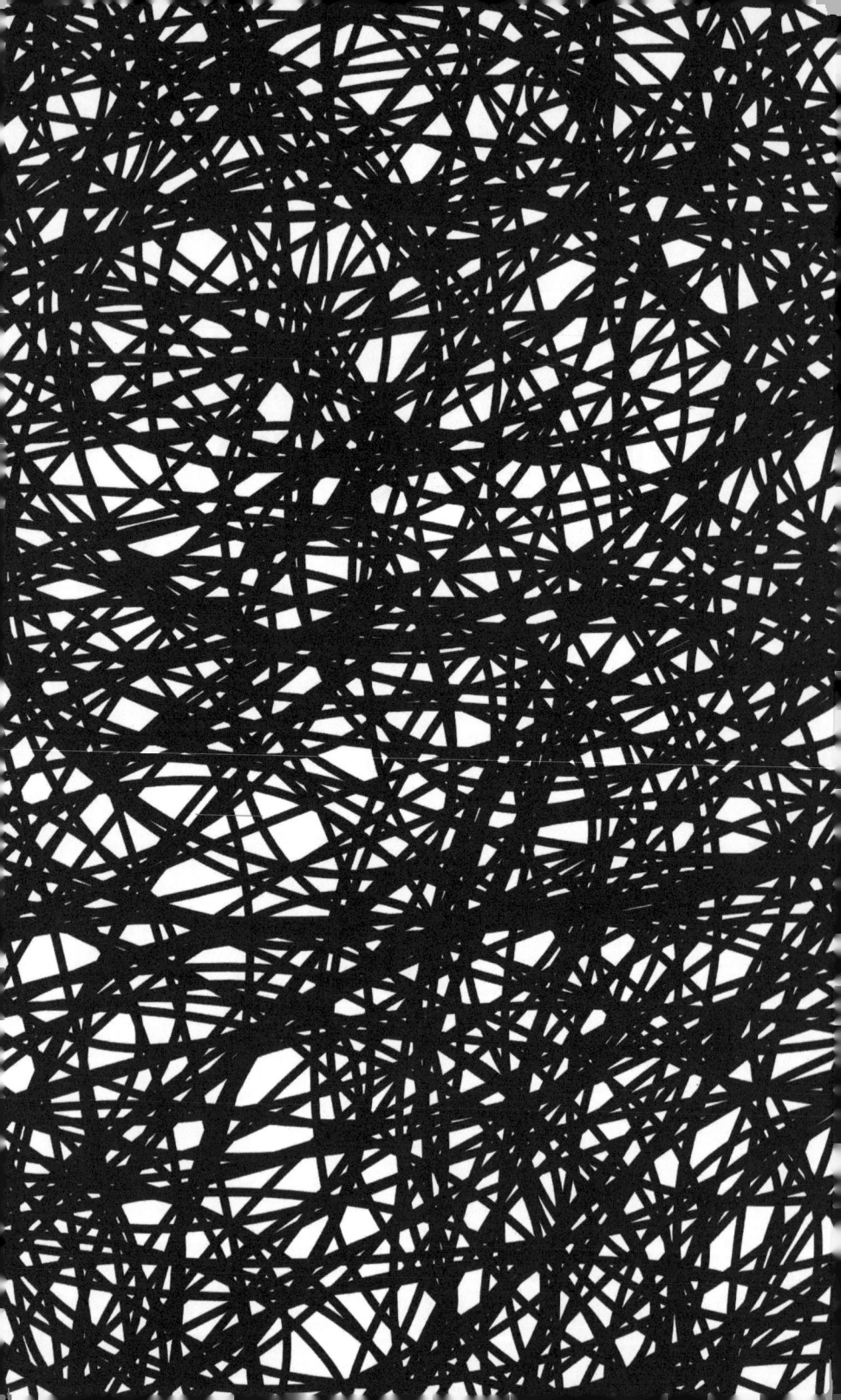

IF YOU STARE INTO THEM LONG ENOUGH, VOIDS TAKE SHAPE.
Once buoyant in absence, you'll find yourself in a colosseum of existence. Silence becomes a symphony and numbness a siege. What was once a vacuum of sensation becomes a thresher of stimulation. Enveloped by relentless pounding, you'll realize you took a step forward. Into the dark. Something you once thought was nothing. Everything that ever was, is, may, not and will flails in front, through and behind you.

Inside the maelstrom of sounds, textures, tastes, and sights, the billowing cosmos will swell. At its zenith, you'll pray to no longer exist. Agonized by reality, you will drop back into a void. You'll assume nihility. That you triumphed to cease.

Then you'll ask: how can nothing comprehend?

In that dreaded cognizance, a pair of eyes will meet you. Yellow and glimmering, they'll find your gaze. Attached to their absence, they'll lurch forward. So gradual in their stride, you'll question if they remain motionless and if you are the approaching entity. Sound returns. A grumble, like a distant train, blossoms gently from the indistinguishable to the corporeal. You will recognize the rumble as it reminds you that fear can be felt on the skin. You have skin. Fragile, vulnerable skin. It's a dog. They're the eyes of a dog and it growls the breath of a dog. Hot and rancid from a life of predation, it'll awaken your bearings of time. Things subsist, before and after. Jagged teeth join the eyes as they invade your space.

Dimension. You take up space. Trivial and fragile space. The beast's aggression explodes into violence, and you will, unfortunately, exist.

THE SOUND OF GLASS BREAKING STARTS IN A DREAM BUT ENDS in reality. Seeing the ceramic shards occupy the same space as her feet transitions Jamie out of her nightmare. There is breath in her lungs and a twinge in her lower back. Awake. Jamie is awake.

"Shit. Ah, shit...Shit!" Jamie proclaims as she adjusts her hips. In order to sit up, Jamie positions her waist to align with her shoulders to avoid spasming a fickle spine. Success. Only a reminder of pain. She gathers her now puzzle of a bowl. Her fingers find the seam from a previous break in the clay. It runs in parallel to the fresh break. Then it comes.

Jamie can set a watch to her own disappointment. The elation of knowing the nightmare is over is always followed by the depression of life. Seeing the superglued crack intersect a new one triggers a chain reaction. The slideshow of memories always leads to now. Sometimes, she doesn't even have to open her eyes to be bombarded by this habitual self-loathing. Just feeling the pillow under her knees can kickstart the cycle.

She has told herself, incalculable times, that she should mentally treat herself better. General consciousness shouldn't harbor such grief. This conclusion is routinely reached and the answer is routinely the same: *Why? What is there to feel okay about?*

Jamie, frazzled to a degree where vision is a conscious decision, grabs a box of cereal from the top of the fridge. She then snags a carton of milk from an empty refrigerator and a bowl that was made for more than one serving of anything. Appropriate bowls are highly valued items, so they are crusted in the filth of meals passed and buried in grime and porcelain at the bottom of the sink. Milk is routinely replenished for the convenience of cereal, so the lone concrete skin lime next to the carton is not indicative of its expiration. She pours the cereal into the bowl and adds the milk. With a dead stare, the milk overflows and she just continues to assault the bowl with lactose. She empties the carton, shakes out the last drops and places it back in the fridge.

Grabbing a spoon, Jamie nestles herself on her stool. Milk has made it to the floor and a steady stream of it rains down from the kitchen island. Transfixed by her bowl of chaos, Jamie gently nudges the bowl toward the end of the table. There's a moment of pause as the bowl teeters off the edge. Finding coffee ring stains under the base triggers Jamie to push her breakfast over the edge.

Jamie grabs her shopworn black denim jacket and slides on laceless flat sneakers. She takes the key ring with only two keys attached, one for a vehicle and one for her apartment door. The other set of keys on the hook is a cluster of metal and plastic trinkets. A marker board calendar hangs above the key hook. Faint and colorful notes are scribbled under a black permanent marker. The black ink is erratically etched over the entire board. After blowing her nose by pressing her thumb against her nostrils, she slams the front door before the ceramic shards stop wobbling.

Nothing quite smells like concrete near an ocean breeze. After a decade of making this walk, it's still a palpable fragrance for Jamie. It's a paradoxical odor. Freshly stale and organically processed are phases she's used to describe it. The shameless scavengers that are seagulls dare not land here and Jamie attributes the stench to their absence. The ocean isn't visible from the short drive, or today's bus ride, from Jamie's apartment, so the smell is always startling. Even if it is stale.

She forgot that the soles of her shoes have been worn down from incessant gear shifting. Every step reminds her as cool air kisses her toes and heels through her exposed socks. The thin fabric now contours with the arch of her foot so breaking into a new pair isn't even a possibility in her mind.

As Jamie walks through this quiet graveyard of gutted semi-trucks, she anxiously punches her knuckles together. It's not hard enough to cause damage, but it's just hard enough to stimulate a driblet of pain. At the end of the lot, a dust-kissed red semi-truck with an equally dust-kissed trailer awaits.

"Okay-dokey," Jamie murmurs over her rhythmic knuckles. She surveys the trailer, walks around the back and settles at the driver's side door. "Alright, not bad. Not bad."

She opens the door and attempts to hoist herself in. Gravity tackles her feet back down to the pavement and a grunt joins the landing. Jamie, to her annoyance, uses the assistant step under the door. *There's no reason I can't do this now.* The memory of needing the step seemingly adds weight to the guilt in her shoulders.

Once inside, Jamie accentuates her last knuckle punch with some extra force. The residual frustration from using the assistant step provides a sharp snip in her hands. Jamie pulls down the visor with one hand and shakes away the pain with the other. There's a photo of a blond six-year-old girl scotch-taped over the mirror. The young girl is sitting on the back step of the truck's trailer. Sighing, Jamie attempts to pull it off and rips the photo in the process.

"Oh, no, no, no, no." She's freed the photo from the visor, but the tear goes between the eyes of the girl . "God damn it." Jamie quickly finds some composure when she uses the tape to patch the photo back together. "Ugh, come on." The moment of victory is cut short by something in her peripherals. An empty bottle of gin sits in her passenger's seat. Jamie fixes the photo back on the visor, grabs the empty bottle and exits the truck.

◼◼◼◼◼◼

Barging into the locker room, Carl perks up at Jamie's dramatic entrance. The towering monster-of-a-man, wearing a black tank top, is quite happy to see a fuming Jamie. "Hey, Jamie. What's shakin'?"

"Have you seen Billy?" Jamie blurts out in a telegraphed effort to appear threatening.

"I'm telling you, either tear into him or report him." Carl looks down to see the empty bottle of gin in Jamie's hand.

"That's the plan."

"Really, because we've had this conversation before."

"Don't be a wiseass. So that's a 'no' on Billy?" Jamie says as she places the bottle on the locker bench.

"Go for Billy" a thin-yet-confident voice says. Billy's a wiry young man with a permanent grin Jamie wants to cut off with a carpenter's knife. He rounds the corner with a bag of trash he ties up in a grocery bag.

"Billy man, what the hell's this?" Jamie asks.

"Looks like a bottle of gin" Billy snarks. He sits down and tosses his grocery bag of trash across the room, missing a trash can. "Rejected!" Billy cackles as he ties his shoes.

"You can't be drinking in my truck, man. This is not the way to deal with a favor."

"Carl drinks in his."

"That's not true but if he did, I'm confident in his ability to drink and drive."

"So was I," Carl interjects.

"It's one thing when you're dickin' around with your own responsibilities but try to give a shit when it's someone else's" Jamie retorts while maintaining eye contact.

Billy takes out a fold of bills and puts it down next to her symbolic gin placement. "Did you want this now?" Jamie's silence solidifies her place in the argument. "And Sally's looking for you."

Jamie grabs the money, walks off and tosses Billy's garbage in the trash on her exit.

"Quiz Wiz at Flanagan's tonight?" Billy asks Carl.

"Why would you even ask me that? No," Carl answers.

Jamie is continually startled by Sally's never-again face. She appears to be in her late forties, but her hands slip on her secret. Bulbous joints that curve away from her thumb. They look ancient. Sally's actual age is somewhere in the middle of her face and hands. A previous hairstyle leaves Sally with a faded purple tint on her conditioned ends. The silver and purple color scheme is unintentionally fetching. She sits behind a waist-high mound of paperwork that presumably has a desk underneath. Wooden sea captain statues are strewn about her office on any available flat surface. Black-fingernailed and wearing a business suit, Sally looks to the knocking upon her open door.

"Hey Jamie, been looking for you" Sally greets with a flip of her hand.

"How's it going? This one's new?" Jamie refers to an unpainted sea captain as she sits down.

"Do teenagers still do drugs?"

"I'm assuming 'yes'," Jamie responds with slight hesitation.

"I feel like they don't."

"Well, I know I did." Jamie takes a moment to appreciate the ocean through the window behind Sally. It's reassuring to place the smell to its source. *Why isn't the sea captain on the windowsill looking out at the ocean? Wouldn't he be looking at the ocean? I guess he'd look at it enough when's he's on the water doing his sea captain duties. Plus, he's an ornament. How visually stimulating would it be to look at the back of a wooden head?"*

"My nephew keeps breaking into houses and smashing street lights."

"Hm? Sorry," Jamie apologizes for pondering on the sea captain. It'll take a moment to re-lubricate her ability to socialize.

"My nephew. He breaks shit." Sally reiterates.

"What does that have to do with drugs?"

"Give him something to do," Sally pitches with a shrug.

"So, to stop your teenage nephew from vandalizing stuff, you're going to introduce him to narcotics?"

"Nothing hard. Weed. Maybe micro-dose him. Don't want him to go on a 'vision quest' or start pitching me crystals to help with menopause or anything of that nature."

"What about, like, sports?"

"The kid's already the school bully. Last thing he needs to be is stronger. Just want to whittle the edges down."

"Then I can't show him how to whittle?" Jamie recommends, pointing to a freshly carved sea captain. It is a work in progress as wooden filings and a whittling knife rest next to it.

"I'm not giving that kid a knife."

"Jesus."

"You'd understand if you met him. Anyway, how are things? I thought you needed some more time off?"

"Ah, no. Everything's...squared away. I guess."

"Really?"

"Yeah."

"You sure? No problem in taking more time."

"...nah, I'm good. We're good," Jamie lies as she rests her elbows on the arms of the chair, letting her knuckles press against each other.

"Oh good. God knows legal battles can go on for eternity."

"Yeah. Things rarely go to litigation."

"Well, here's another thing. What's your tomorrow like?"

"It can be clear."

"What if it's double-double for 983 miles."

"Crystal."

Sally smirks from Jamie's wordplay. "Well, hear this first. It's pay by load."

"Freight?"

"Nah, your truck's enough."

"Then if I leave tomorrow, I can make it before ten on Thursday."

"The last two hundred-ish miles are off the beaten path in Connecticut, so it may take an extra minute."

"Alright, as long as I'm not hauling fetuses."

"Far from it."

"Birth control?"

"Construction materials and fancy bread."

"Fancy bread?"

"An upstart bakery is trying to expand and they manufacture fancy bread machinery here."

"Huh. Will it be ready by tomorrow?"

"Fancy bread'll be baked by dawn and machinery packed by ten. Your truck good to go? Any problems with Billy?"

"....no. He's fine. We're good...again. Everything's good," Jamie putters the words out as she gets up from her seat. Sally's focus was on tracking paperwork, so she missed Jamie failing to get out of the chair in her first attempt.

"Hey, an FYI before you step out," Sally interjects as she keeps her eyes on paperwork.

"Yeah?"

"I'm having their office sign your logbook."

"What's that supposed to do?"

"To see if it adds up."

"I thought we were past this."

"Put an ELD in your truck," Sally remarks with eye contact.

"Not a fan of that idea."

"Then enjoy the scrutiny," and Sally goes back to paperwork.

Jamie pauses in the doorway. "Things coming early really that big of an issue?"

"Not after menopause."

"Ah, there's a crystal for that," Jamie barbs on her exit.

Jamie walks out of the office to see Carl in his jacket, slinging a duffel bag over his shoulder.

"Hey hey," Carl chirps with an authentic glee. "You doing the Connecticut thing?"

"Yeah, I'm on. Why didn't you take it?" Jamie asks.

"Separate gig."

"Ah."

"But guess what? Albany," Carl asks.

"Hey, tomorrow?" Jamie matches his enthusiasm and the two exit the building into the loading bay.

Dead. Dead and grey are the usual, but the rain-pregnant skies tinted this loading bay with an especially arid coldness. If Jamie wasn't so distracted, she may have noticed its sterile hue. Subtle, but impossible.

"Mmm hmm, and you know what that means we can do?" Carl pitches.

"Come on, you kept up with that. I have to catch my breath after I put on socks." Jamie responds as Billy passes them.

"Hey hey hey, you back on the roster?" Billy says.

"Tomorrow morning." Jamie's response takes some mental fortitude.

"Good for you. I know you needed it."

"Ugh...thanks," Jamie responds through coiled lips.

"Carl, you up for a—"

"You can go ahead and stop talking to me" Carl throws away toward Billy.

"Alright...," Billy continues on as a hushed "Fuckster," babbles from his mouth.

"Hey, he—"

"I heard him," Carl intercepts Jamie's defense and keeps his head forward.

Still fazed by the interaction, Jamie turns to see Billy's back.

"If he got sidelined by a bus, I wouldn't have an opinion. It would be like hearing about the weather," Carl continues on to the lagging Jamie.

"Ah, hopefully some life experience will round out those douche ends a bit," Jamie adds.

"He didn't hesitate to hop on your situation, so those edges are concrete. Fuck that dude."

"I needed money. He paid me," Jamie retorts.

"If Sally didn't ride him, that money woulda' went to the tow yard."

"I mean, I don't know."

"I do," Carl says as Jamie turns to Billy "Eh, but who knows? I'm being unfair. Maybe getting his shit repo'd is the kick in the ass that'll even him out."

REALITY SQUALL | 9

Billy enters the locker room and enters what seems to be an upside-down exterior of a tall grass field. Gravity still persists, and when Billy steps into an area of alternate physics, he falls up to the ground.

The door closes accompanied by a distant and muffled yelp. Startled by the phenomenon, seen on the edge of her eye, Jamie whips back. She stands in awe of what she may have just witnessed. She looks to Carl for support, but he's oblivious to the potential anomaly. Sally exits the same door Billy entered and the office is seemingly normal.

"Wait, really?" a dazed Jamie whispers in the air.

"Oh, fuck no, he'll be president one day," Carl answers the forgotten question.

Jamie shakes off her trance and continues on.

JAMIE HAS A CAR BUT HASN'T STARTED ITS ENGINE IN TWO months. It's twelve years old and the current battery's been under the hood eight of those twelve. She told herself to start it after two weeks, but the exertion to get there from her bed would have been too taxing. That and she doesn't know how much gas is left in the tank. She has a looming suspicion that she could make it to a gas station, but the remaining gasoline would be on the brink of stale. The missing gas cap pretty much guarantees it.

The walk from Sally's lot to Jamie's apartment is a little over three miles. The majority of the space is highway and grass, but there is a small cluster of fast food restaurants next to an off-ramp. Jamie took the bus to Sally's but decided to walk back to her apartment. Needing stimuli that's not her ceiling and avoiding cleaning the milk off the floor, Jamie trudges to the side of the road. *I'm out of breath. I'm out of breath walking on flat land.*

The beacon of fast food stands proudly in the distance. *Oh, thank god,* Jamie thinks. It is an opportunity to not only rest but to hydrate. That's all. That's the plan. Drink a liter of water and sit for ten minutes before walking the rest of the way home. *And maybe just a side of fries.* Just a snack, some water, and a quick break. *Maybe a large fries, I burned some calories on the walk and will continue to walk.* She skipped breakfast so the plan remains largely the same.

The blood in Jamie's exhausted legs is now her stomach. Going from empty to a double cheeseburger, 25 ounce soda and two large fries is an all hands on deck scenario for Jamie's digestive tract. She stands to throw her food away but immediately sits back in her booth. The lack of blood flowing into her skull dissolves the floor under her feet. She lands hard enough that the entire booth shifts a little more than an inch. The hard, laminated plastic does not sit well with her spine. Rigid and unforgiving, her lower back shifts into a precarious position. Free of pain at the moment, she knows pain is stalking her next movement. Desperate for hydration, Jamie drinks her concoction of melting ice and diluted soda.

It's less than a mile. If I can get through the nerve pangs of standing up, walking will ease my back into a better spot. Get up. 1,2,3, up!...Okay....3,2,1,up! It's going to get worse before it gets better. Less than a mile and I can lie down for as long as I want. Right into the morning. You can do it. 3,2,1—

"Thanks and have a good rest of your day," Jamie tells her cab driver.

"Mm," the man replies without turning his head.

Jamie shimmies her body to the edge of the musty leather seat. With the cab door open, all she would have to do is lean forward and let gravity take her feet to the pavement. Jamie's been strategizing this maneuver the entire car ride. The entire four-minute ride.

"You al'ight?" the cabbie asks about the prolonged sound of squeaking leather.

"Oh yeah, just give me a minute," Jamie responds, positioning herself to fall out of her seat. Jamie looks down at the asphalt and positions her feet to land. She's going to rotate out of the seat so she has to keep her feet at an obtuse angle.

Holding her breath, she pivots forward. Success. She stands straight up and closes the door. The cab is gone as soon as the door lock sets.

She can walk. The walk from the sidewalk to her apartment steps is tight, but the thirty feet alleviates some of the pain. A frail thought buried in her gloom regrets not walking the rest of the way. If thirty feet could help, what would a mile do?

"Oof," Jamie blurts at the sour stench. Since she's low on paper towels and they're being used as toilet paper, Jamie ends up with a bath towel to sop up the literal spilled milk. Wringing it out over her stack of dishes reveals a few sticky curds in the cloth. She was considering throwing this towel away and that milk solids solidify that idea.

Under the sink, a bagless trashcan overflows with paper trash. Jamie pulls the entire trash can out to rest on the kitchen floor. Strategy is at its finest as she flops the lactose-moistened towel onto the can and stomps it down. The towel turns out to be a convenient compaction device. It encases paper trash so only one Styrofoam container rolls off the pile. Jamie picks up the garbage to find a piece of yellow processed cheese welded onto its edge. She can't remember what meal this was or when she ate it. Jamie doesn't hesitate to pry the crusty cheese from its polystyrene box and slips it into her mouth. It doesn't even feel like a conscious decision. Just something as rote as brushing her teeth.

Jamie is on the brink of being a hoarder. Newspapers, magazines, and legal documents are stacked in every corner. Cleanliness isn't totally abandoned, but filth is strategically compartmentalized. Even with a full dishwasher, plates and glasses stay stacked in the sink. Laundry has long reached maximum capacity and her hamper is invisible under a mountain of clothes. Jamie's been using the clutter of laundry as her closet. She wears whatever the least-wrinkled piece of clothing is and then returns it to the pile upon the day's completion.

On her living room couch, Jamie uses the last of her superglue to mend the bowl she shattered. The fractures look as if they're a part of the bowl's design now. From several incidents, there's barely space where a crack isn't present. She clears some space on her coffee table and places it on a flat surface. It wobbles but its purpose as a bowl remains intact. Picking it up, she inspects her job. Specks of dog hair are embedded in the glue. The sight brings her memories, and the memories bring her pause.

She looks to a pristine dog bed where her living room meets the kitchen tile. "Agh...fuck." Jamie sighs, finding a divot on the couch next to her. The groove is riddled with dog hair and Jamie runs her hand over the imprint. It sinks so low she can feel the springs of the pullout bed. "Yup..." Jamie stands and takes her avant-garde bowl to her bedroom. "...fuck." On her way to the disaster area of her bedroom, she punches her knuckles together passing a completely vacant second bedroom. No bed. No curtains. Just four walls and a window. She used to stand in its doorway and punch her knuckles raw. She's gotten to the place where she merely walks by. She does always catch a glimpse of the north facing wall, however. On that wall, there are shapeless scribbles of varying colors about four feet off the ground.

Jamie lays in her bed and stares at the ceiling. She rolls to her side and looks towards her curtains. Between the conjoining fabric; the void of night. Closing her eyes compels her legs to walk. Much like her morning wave of depression, heading to the bathroom around 2:00 a.m. is practically a ritual. This is an action only motivated by boredom. Her head usually meets her pillow by 11:37 p.m. so that's roughly three hours of attempting to sleep while calculating the time before her alarm. Five hours of sleep is becoming infamous and five hours of quality sleep is mythic.

Coming to terms with her spring-loaded eyelids, Jamie sits up and heads to the bathroom. Her soap and moisturizers have been depleted but a one-gallon shampoo bottle with a plastic jug pump is up for the task of overall cleanliness. A shower was in the back of her mind but seeing the absence of a towel cancels any hopes of bathing. She can see the cardboard of the paper towel roll as well. The safety net of her discarded toilet paper in the trash is also depleted. Not that mucus hardened tissues are a deliberate backup plan, but they have saved the day in the past. This alerts Jamie to save any significant toilet endeavors for Sally's bathroom in a few hours.

Rarely does Jamie not take her shirt off in the bathroom. Looking back at herself in the mirror was an exercise aimed with positive intent. Now, it is justification for her disgust. With her attention focused on her flaws, she starts to punch her knuckles. *My god. I have to be a human like this. My hair. It's what a witch's hair would be like. Dry on the scalp, scraggily in the middle and oily at the ends. My head's a fucking paradox. And stretch marks. Stretch marks for days. I got some, got rid of some and now I'm mostly stretch marks. I don't have an excuse anymore.* The impact causes a ripple in her stomach and thus intensifies her self-flagellation. *Your tit flesh jiggles you fat piece of shit.* Jamie's focus is entirely on her physique as the power behind her strikes increases. *Not even your actual tit, but the flabby fucking flesh by your shoulder.* Passed the point of bruising but right before the bone is broken, her alarm goes off in the bedroom. *How'd you gain weight in that specific place on your dumpy-* The alarm saves her a hospital visit and interrupts her self-deprecation.

Jamie grabs her phone and turns off the alarm. Something about the time raises an eyebrow. *8:00 a.m?* There are plenty of reasons behind an incorrect phone, but what about the sun? Shuffling over to the curtains, Jamie closes her eyes tight to troubleshoot for answers. This could be a trick of the iris. The sudden change from a lit bathroom to a dark bedroom? She opens her eyes. The fabric is highlighted by the morning light.

Jamie opens the curtains. The sun has been up for quite some time and Jamie is left wondering how that's possible. She steps out of her bedroom and looks into her hallway. Light from the windows of the vacant bedroom shines on the floor. Jamie steps back into her bedroom. She feels exhausted, but she convinces herself this is how she usually feels. Jamie looks at her mountain of laundry. Not only does she have to find something to wear for today, but for at least a week.

Clawing her way through the pile, she has cultivated a nice heap of wardrobes that won't offend anyone by their odor. She then continues to dig. Her bedroom floor becomes more laundry than carpet, but she finds it. At the bottom of her wicker hamper, a duffel bag sits crumpled next to underwear that would offend pretty much anyone. She pulls out the duffel bag and puts it next to her pile of clothes on the bed. "Oh, boy." Opening it, she finds a long forgotten long sleeve shirt, socks that could chip a tooth if bitten into and a ziplock bag of toiletries.

"Hey, hey," mutters Jamie. Inside the bag, an almost full roll of deodorant, a travel tube of toothpaste, a bottle of gummy vitamins, travel mouthwash, and two toothbrushes. One toothbrush is used to the point where the discolored bristles have sprawled away from each other. The other is a child's toothbrush. It's short with firm multicolored bristles. Jamie unzips the bag and removes the kid's toothbrush. She attempts to break it in half, but its stout shape gives it a sturdy foundation. Failing to snap the brush, Jamie merely tosses it into the bottom of the hamper and buries it under soiled clothes.

———

"How'd you sleep?" Sally asks in the same exact outfit as yesterday, but noticeably less wrinkled.

"...I think well," Jamie answers to the middle space.

"You sure?"

Jamie sees that Sally is investigating her mental state. For the safety of her job, Jamie forces her eyes not to roll back "It's been a while. They're managed. I'm good."

"Okay. You look good."

"I do?"

"You've looked worse. Insurance won't keep replacing windows and bandaging you up, so if you're going to have one of your sleepy spells, let me know."

"'Spells?' I don't need to regain my composure under the willow tree after a sudden case of the vapors" Jamie says with a lazy southern drawl.

"How about fits?"

"I can do fits."

"Fits it is."

"But it's been a quite some time. They're under control."

Jamie's frail smirk is rewarded by a hard long stare from Sally "...alight. This is new." Sally motions to a large dent on the grill of Jamie's truck. "It anything under the hood?"

"Don't know. Didn't catch it until now."

"Billy?" asks Sally.

"Ah, shit. Yeah, I guess."

"I can dock him next time I see him," Sally remarks as she scribbles a note on her clipboard.

"Let me see if it's an issue first."

"Why I like one person per truck. Easier to track, less drama."

"Didn't want to, just needed the money."

"I mean, I get it. Other than that, you're all set."

Jamie tries to end the walk around and grips onto the driver's side door. Sally interrupts her departure.

"Hold up, scratch that, just one last thing...," Sally checks off, dates, and signs one of the many check points in her logbook. "Here you go." Separating her notes from the logbook, Sally offers the leatherbound ledger to Jamie.

"Aw, yeah...almost forgot," Jamie sighs as she grabs the book.

"No you didn't."

"I wanted to," Jamie says as she opens the truck door.

"Be safe."

"Thanks. Seriously, and see you—" Jamie fails to hoist herself into the driver's seat.

"Need a hand?"

"Nope, just ah-just...I'm...," Jamie uses the assistant step and settles into her seat "fine." She holds her breath to avoid showing Sally she's out of shape.

"Alright then, happy trails."

"Yeah," Jamie exhales and slams the door. Finding her rhythm, Jamie keeps her labored breath through her nose as she nods to Sally. Not an easy effort as her left nostril is clogged.

As Jamie settles into her seat, she looks at the torn picture of the girl on the visor.

After a deep exhale, she presses the clutch pedal down and starts the truck. The truck gently rumbles as if a drummer started rehearsing in the engine. Jamie reaches under her seat. She finds her blue dented thermos, unscrews the top and whiffs the remnants.

"Whoa, hey, maybe." Jamie sips from the discarded thermos and nods "Mmm hmm, okay, that's what I'm talking about." She takes another sip and retrieves an aluminum sheet of prescription pills from her glove compartment. 'Mmm hmm, mmm hmm, mmm hmm." She pries two out of their packaging and uses the remaining liquid from the thermos to knock them back.

Tossing the thermos on the driver's seat, Jamie embraces her cockpit. It's inconceivable the same person that drives this truck sleeps in that bedroom. *One day, I'll take care of myself like I take care of my truck* is a lie Jamie liked to repeatedly tell herself. Not only is there a lack of litter, but there is a lack of evidence if there ever being litter. Cupholders are free of ring stains from drinks past, the fabric floormats are clear of lint or dust and the normal unbleached dashboard is as dark and carries the same sheen as the first day she stepped in. The difference between the interior and the exterior is staggering. For a twelve-year-old vehicle, one could assume this was in storage until this very day. The truck on the inside is a radically different truck from the one the world can see.

Jamie sits back, giving herself over to the hug of the chair. Her hands rest on the steering wheel, making contact with the vinyl resin one finger at a time. Before her foot touches the accelerator, her buttock finds the well-earned groove in her seat. Whatever nagging back pain she was experiencing outside of the truck washes away like nausea after vomiting. Granted, her spine reverted to a mild form of scoliosis, but it is a conditioned and somehow relieving aliment.

Glancing across the gauges, Jamie practices the ten gears on her stick shift. The truck hisses as air is supplied to the compression brake. This instinctively alerts Jamie to take her foot off the brake. This is it. The highest level of homeostasis. Jamie's heart rate goes down and her pupils dilate. Her universe is the confines of this truck. There is only one goal and she is fully prepared to execute her mission with extreme competence. The sole of her shoe touches the pedal and the soul of the engine hums. She turns the wheel and seventy-three thousand pounds follow her.

The windshield's display of concrete and truck innards drops off to the expanse of the open road. The unending sky is clear and awaits her travels. With an exhausted breath, Jamie looks on: "Oh, boy," she says.

Shortly after a stretch of a dilapidated factory town, Jamie finds herself surrounded by greenery. Encased by the outstretched pine, Jamie's anxieties remain present but are manageable. Driving takes up just enough of her focus to hush her gnawing consciousness in a blanket of repetition. Jamie shares the road with a fair amount of traffic, but the pit stops are far and few between.

Most truckers fill that surplus of mental bandwidth with satellite radio. Having your entertainment curated leaves room for your brain to sync into a state of flow. Awareness can be a detriment as time can become a harsh warden to the endurance of the profession. Jamie doesn't listen to anything. Her state of flow could become so intense, she could drive for hours past her destination. She had a surplus of mental fiber to masticate her way through any journey.

Jamie sits alone at a bustling truck stop diner. She's in the certified trucker section while the country buffet is stationed in the civilian area. Roadside buffets are a fairly predictable affair. Twenty-four hour breakfasts along with some kind of chicken-fried steak, mashed potatoes that were maybe mashed before they were chemically dehydrated and reduced to a unrecognizable powder, pink slabs of jerky labeled "ham," dinner rolls to service the bowl of prepackaged whipped butter in melting ice and a garishly tinted pile of room temperature green beans floating in frothy water.

The sun is still in the sky, so Jamie has the willpower to be above the buffet. With her own hoggle of coffee, Jamie looks down at the remnants of an appetizer sampler. An empty bottle of ketchup sits beside an empty glass of soda and Jamie stirs the remaining ice. Melted just enough to get half a cup of diluted cola, Jamie finishes off the liquid through her straw. A waitress comes over and places a burger and fries in front of Jamie along with a side of pancakes.

"Thank you, and can I get a refill when you get a chance?" With a vacant nod, the waitress grabs the glass. Jamie reaches out to the booth behind her to grab a second bottle of ketchup as the waitress walks off.

Seeing only one prepackaged butter, Jamie looks for the waitress and finds the swaying grey doors to the kitchen. No avail at the booth behind her either. Jamie's palm told her the pancakes were hot enough for the extra butter to not just melt between the cakes, but also atop the stack. Swallowing her pride so she can swallow her meal, Jamie gets up and maneuvers herself around the retractable belt stanchions. Failing to fit between the wall and the barricade, Jamie unclasps the belt and gets to the ice bowl of dairy. She covertly grabs a few with a couple of coffee creamers as collateral damage.

Sliding back into her booth, an abrupt sense of euphoria cuddles her psyche. She doesn't know why, but she embraces the gift from her brain. Ease. A flicker of nebulous reassurance. It's like hearing a song she forgot used to be her favorite. Looking up from her heist, she's makes eye contact with the polo shirt-wearing manager. Her sporadic smile melts away from the shame. The manager couldn't care less about the creamer.

———

A young woman in a shopworn black peacoat, sunglasses, and a long brim fedora hitchhikes on the outskirts of the diner's parking lot. She has a black leather backpack attached to her and is contact juggling a glass ball in her free hand.

Not a hitchhiker, Jamie suspects. Maybe a freeder walking between friend's homes but not a lifer. Nah, probably not even a freeder. She has a home. She doesn't have that dusty brown/ black disheveled thing going on. Clothes are too maintained. Maybe there's a festival nearby that she's on her way to. Or maybe a breakup. Yeah. Big old break up and she walked out on him or her because she caught him or her with her very own best friend who is also a him or he-

A blaring horn cuts through Jamie's reverie.

"Whoop! Shit!" Jamie whips to see that she's drifting dangerously close to a landscaping truck. After correcting her course, Jamie looks toward the tattered truck brimming with rusted gardening tools. The landscaper, eating a sandwich in one hand and on his smart phone in the other, inaudibly yells toward Jamie.

"Sorry! Sorry," Jamie says as the pickup passes her. "Ugh, fuck me." This is why Jamie doesn't listen to satellite radio. She drives past the wayward hitchhiker. Exiting the lot, Jamie joins the freeway.

Jamie parks her truck onto the freight scale. As the sun sets behind the stop sign, it obscures the traffic light in shadow. She can only tell it was lit because of the slight contrast between the orange of the sun and the red of the stop light. Everything else is a silhouette. Jamie sips from her thermos and waits for the results. As she waits, she catches a glint from a black speck moving across the sky. In front of the sun, it is hard to gauge its shape or velocity. Much like a distant plane, it looks motionless in the sky. But it must be moving because it closes in on the edge of the setting sun.

A quick flicker of shadow races across her vehicle from the small, shapeless body. While the speck flew across the horizon, the station light must have turned green. Jamie didn't physically see her approval, but she apparently makes weight. She looks at her logbook. It's crammed in the side compartment of the driver's side door. It would say to stop driving in two hours and twelve minutes. Spiteful to its presence, Jamie becomes emboldened to continue onward.

Jamie shifts into second gear but keeps the clutch down. A large batch of air exhales deep from her lungs. She flips her visor down. *Maybe one day, I can love myself a fraction as much as I love*-Lost reflecting on the photo of her child, the light turns green from red. She sees it this time. Momentarily confused by the déjà vu , Jamie looks toward the sky for some reaffirmation. Whatever that speck was, it's gone.

The sun kisses the thick tree line. Night creeps its way from the horizon, clamoring for Jamie and her truck. Already forgetting the potential anomaly, Jamie flips the visor up and exits the weigh station.

Night cascades the blacktop and headlights pierce through the night onto the vacant road. The sight of mile marker 121 informs Jamie to grab the CB radio dangling overhead. The green signs get harder to see every year as New Jersey's pine-barrens gradually expand their lush dominion.

"Irwar-ack...Jeezus. Hup! Ha! Jeeeeezus...motherrrrrr fuc-cccking JESUS!" Jamie warms her voice as she hasn't spoken for several hours. Some quick vulgarity in varied volumes is a dependable lubricant for vocal cords. With a grip on the receiver and a rotation of the shoulder, Jamie speaks.

"Ironhide, this is Gamey Jamie, what's your 20?" Jamie asks through the receiver.

"Hey hey Gamey, nice to have you back. I'm rollin' in on Pic-A-Lilli's," Carl's voice crackles back.

"Be there in thirty."

"Yeehaw, 10-4 good buddy."

"10-4" Jamie hangs up the radio and continues her drive. The CB radio chimes her name.

"Jamie?" a woman's voice cracks through the static. Confused, Jamie stares at the receiver. As her eyes dart back and forth between the radio and the road, she decides not to respond. "Gamey Jamie?" Jamie grabs the receiver and licks her lips. This moment feels precarious, as if she were about to flirt with a wanted criminal.

"Go for Jamie." Silence is the only response, so she tries again. "...go for Jamie."

"Hahahahah!" Harsh yet genuine female laughter cackles through the weak speaker.

"Hello? What's your handle?"

"Hahahahah...ohhhhh...," the laughter dies down as the operator recomposes herself. "She's not from Ohio, Jamie. She's not even a person."

"Hello. Get back to me," Jamie responds, doing her best to project professionalism. Again, silence is the only response. "Last time, over."

"...." Nothing.

In a burst of energy, Jamie hikes her receiver back up and grabs her thermos. She unscrews the lid while holding the canister between her thighs. She swigs its contents and then fastens the lid back on. "Oh boy, today."

3

EVEN IN THE CLOUD-RIDDLED SKY, THE MOON'S BRIMMING effervescence reflects off the tree tops. It's the thinnest of twinkles, but it envelops the pine in the cleanest of glows. In between the bark, artificial light begins to bleed through as Jamie descends further down the road. A restaurant that looks like it was once a part of a shanty town illuminates the roadside. The neon sign flickers a repugnant cocktail of colors that even moths avoid. Made out of rotten wood and rusted beer signs, the Pic-A-Lilli Inn is home to bikers, truckers, and nothing in between.

Shifting gears, Jamie gyrates her hips, shoulders and neck. She flexes her toes and attempts to bring sensation back to her left foot. Both of her shoulders crack when she stretches them, but her left would cause a chiropractor to raise an eyebrow. Tingling with sensation, yet still blunt, Jamie's left foot successfully changes gears.

The same visual spectacle the moon provides to the trees extends to semi-trailers. In a long row of trucks, Jamie spots a void within the glinting moonlight. For being a supposed trucker's paradise, the Pic-A-Lilli Inn is an obstacle course for anything with an engine. The truck lot is too small and ends about eight feet too close to the actual Inn. For the price of alcohol, Jamie is continually amazed someone hasn't backed into their kitchen. Rotating her head back and forth to stimulate blood flow to her still sleeping foot, Jamie pulls her keys from the ignition. It takes time to safely walk. Too much time.

A friend would be concerned, so it's best Jamie's alone. On her way to the entrance, she uses an adjacent trailer as support while her left foot remembers how to be an appendage.

The wooden interior of Pic-A-Lilli's is coated in a thin film of grease and tabletops are littered with fragments of meals past. For all its striking sights and smells, the noise is fairly low. This is not the end destination for any of their clientele, so music is projected right below speaking volume and conversations don't go past the table. Dulled neon beer signs act as the primary source of iridescent light and the floorboards would fail a health and safety inspection on the first step. Multicolored and warped, if you stare at the floor long enough you may induce a sense of vertigo.

Jamie walks in and is immediately overtaken by a euphoric blanket of normalcy. Pic-A-Lilli's is a part of her routine, and the dull sounds sync her back into that security.

"Yo-to-you, my man," Carl stands up at a corner table and approaches Jamie with wide arms.

"Hey hey!" Jamie exclaims. The two hug and Carl is strong enough to hoist Jamie off the ground.

"Uh, oh, argh. My back!" Carl fakes a back injury upon Jamie's release.

"Ah, you piece of shit," Jamie barbs.

"Ha, ehhhh, let's go fuck up our cholesterol."

Jamie and Carl sit across from each other while a dwindling bowl of chicken wings sit next to a swelling bowl of bones. A stack of well-used playing cards and a small bundle of twigs sit next to the empty salt and pepper shakers.

The first thing Jamie notices about Carl is that he's continued to take care of himself in her absence. Maybe it's the contrast to his denim vest or the way the punk rock neon complements his coffee complexion, but he looks healthy. His arms are powerful and not like a fitness model or a bodybuilder. He's primarily made of solid, practical muscle. His face follows suit. Jamie remembers the bloodshot and putrid yellow in Carl's eyes. No more. Now they're pristine and his cheeks are retaining water instead of flimsily keeping his face on his skull.

"So, I got myself some water weights," Carl proclaims in between bites.

"Aren't those, for like, pregnant women in pools?"

"Not the shit that floats, but something you fill with water and throw around. Keeps the weight down in my load."

"Hm, 'shit that floats'."

"It's from the fat."

"What?"

"In the toilet. Poop that's full of grease floats. Healthy poop sinks."

"Huh. I don't think mine ever sank."

"Mmm hmm, metaphor for life really."

"Substance has weight."

"Pfft, sure." As Carl peels the meat off his chicken wing, Jamie sees something familiar in the corner of her eye. "But who the hell knows, right? Remember when they told us to eat like ninety-seven servings of bread a day. That food pyramid shit is pretty much the opposite of what you're supposed to do."

"That poster littered my high school's walls." The woman that was hitchhiking earlier today is sitting at the bar. She's sipping away on a glass of whiskey as she stencils on a napkin. Her peacoat remains on but her hat rests on her knees. Her dyed hair is shaved, but has grown in about a half an inch. This gave her scalp an illusory effect. Her natural color is blonde, but her tips are as black as dye can get. Her left foot sways gently as it dangles off the stool. She reaches into her bag and swaps out her pencils for a marker. Checking under the cap, she decides against the color and rifles through a fistful of markers before she picks another. She quickly streaks the felt against the back of her hand, ponders on the width and color on her skin and tosses the drawing utensils back into her bag. She then returns to her picturesque posture on her bar stool.

"You ever do this? Corkscrew the bones off with your fingers and then just eat the meat?" Carl pulls the bones from his chicken wing and presents them to a distracted Jamie. "It's a little tricky to get the second bone off, but eating the whole wing at once is a fucking trip."

"Huh? Sorry." Hypnotized by the woman's pendulous leg, Jamie returns to Carl's attention. Carl turns to see what Jamie is staring at. "I saw her hitching on the 206 earlier. Must have got a ride."

"Or she's really fast," Carl quips.

"Just a peculiar lookin' hitch."

"Probably in a rut and needs a ride. Found her boyfriend going down on the mailman and walked out on him or something."

"Needs a ride to her parents in Hartford but the car's under his name?"

"Exactly, writing down what she's going to say to him when getting her stuff."

"Or what she's going to say to her," Jamie adds.

"Oooooh," Carl blares while simultaneously chewing.

"Yeah, how about that," Jamie jokingly nods.

"I think we got it. We got it, right? I think we got it."

"Oh yeah, no need to ask her anymore, really," Jamie's giggle dies down. A pleasant silence slinks through the booth while a few bones are added to the pile.

"Speaking of parents, how's your mum," Carl asks.

"Not bad. Supportive, which I could use."

"Yeah?"

"Yeah," Jamie earnestly answers. It feels like a lie, but it is a bright spot of reassurance. Jamie didn't recognize it until she said it aloud.

"Always liked her. Good mum, your mum."

"Yeah, she's a good grandma. I'm not sure how step-grandmothers work."

"If Kimmy wants to see her, she'll get to see her. Right?"

"'At the discretion of the plaintiff'" Jamie orates to an empty bowl of sauce and chicken grease.

"Is he really that much of a dick?"

"Yeah...no. It may just take some time."

"Keep cracking away at it. It'll right itself once the chaos settles."

"That's the plan."

"She going to keep drumming?" Carl asks.

"I'm not sure. Think she's on pause."

"Raw tenacity like that, she can be the next Keith Moon."

"Who?" Through Jamie's furrowed brow, a proud smirk slinks its way across her face.

"Exactly. I'm stepping out for a smoke. Coming?"

"You can smoke E-Cigarettes in here."

" I know…" Carl pulls out an electric cigarette from his vest pocket. Jamie notices his shoulders again. He loads in a cartridge of scented vapor. "Still like the habit of stepping outside. Plus, folks don't like the smell of "fresh-baked brownie" vapor when they're eating actual food."

"I always got cranky looks when I smoked indoors or vaped or whatever. I'm good though, thanks," Jamie answers as she motions to her water. Guilt springs in her gut when she hopes he'd leave soon. Solidarity keeps the glasses filled with plain H2O but she could get another four hours on the road if she got the boost that comes after a beer.

Carl steps out of his booth. "Copy that. Back in a minute."

As Carl walks away, Jamie's line of sight returns to the woman at the bar. The envy toward her drink found a stockpile of separate grievousness. She just looks natural. Nothing in regards to vanity but in regards to just how together she looks. Her wardrobe, her posture, and the space around her looks as if they are supposed to be there. Jamie never believed she belonged anywhere. But she thought she was a good mother. One of the few things she didn't have to try to be good at. She gets out of her seat.

As soon as Jamie steps into the single occupancy bathroom, the light turns on from a motion sensor. It's shockingly clean with a healthy amount of toilet paper atop the tank. Instinctively, Jamie takes her shirt off and hangs it on the small castle of toilet paper.

Jamie sits on the toilet and takes a deep breath. It takes some effort, but she avoids crying. She rests her thumb and index fingers on her eyelashes to aid in keeping her eyes closed. Maybe this was too soon. The thought slithers through her skull. A brief flash of laughter with Carl yields to but I liked that and it happened. You can't take that away. That, plus a deep breath, puts a halt to the tears. Lowering her hands, Jamie finds the bathroom graffiti.

A crude stick figure, erratically scribbled in a black sharpie with highlighter yellow eyes, is sketched on the bathroom wall. The question "Can you see it?" is etched under it in both sharpie and highlighter. Jamie's hand can reach the wall and the drawing is at her eye level. Whatever crazy person drew this, they did it on the toilet. Transfixed by the image, she notices that the aggressive streaks of black aren't connected. The artist didn't just scribble like a toddler in a coloring book. They individually drew every line—but there are hundreds. Jamie has never seen a sharpie run out of ink, but this singular doodle could have emptied one.

The lights go out from the lack of movement and Jamie waves her hands to reactivate the sensor. "Ah, come on," Jamie yelps. The quick scare motivates her to start wiping.

After she finishes wiping and puts on her shirt, Jamie ponders to herself. She peeks down toward the bowl. Through her thighs, she's curious to see the buoyancy of her feces. Before she gets a glimpse, the lights go out again. In that moment of darkness, orange dog-eyes stare at her. They're located right over the eyes of the sketched stick man. Jamie is unaware that she is being watched but exclaims "shit!" as she waves for the lights to turn back on.

The light returns but Jamie waves to reactivate a motion sensor that doesn't exist. She's seated at her booth and there's no wraith-like dog to meet her. "Uh! Ah!" Dumbfounded by the teleportation, Jamie leaves her hand in the air. "Uhhhhh" she moans as her eyes adjust to the contrast in lighting. Slowly, she places her hands on the table top. "Ummmmm" and the hum continues on after her mouth closes.

No one seems to be staring at her. You would think the lapse of physics would attract some eyes. The woman at the bar though. She's smiling while making direct eye contact. Jamie's stares back at her. Her eyes are wide and her lips tremble. Her beer is at the same level, but does that mean anything?

How much more beer could you drink in the time it takes to walk back from the bathroom? Jamie nods in an attempt to simulate something one would consider normal. The girl at the bar motions, with a little flourish of the wrist, for Jamie to look down. Jamie obliges.

"Ah, fuckin' shit," Jamie says in a descending volume. Her pants are still around her ankles. In a dash of desperation, Jamie pulls her pants up with little decorum and even less stealth. She looks around to make sure no one sees her exposed ass and crotch. "Holy mother of fuck," Jamie whispers to herself. Thank god I wiped.

She looks back at the woman at the bar. She's turned back around and continues to scribble. However, her foot stopped swinging. It's now fixed on the bottom rung of her stool. For some reason, this made her presence less intoxicating and more insidious. Even with vague feelings of dread, Jamie keeps her eyes on her in an odd fixation. Should I talk to her-

"Yo-ho-ho," Carl returns from his vaping.

Jamie snaps out of her daze when Carl enters her line of sight "Dah, ah, hey."

"Some insensitive ass-hat turned the bathroom into a crime scene."

"What?"

"Some dude didn't flush."

"Oh..." Jamie rottenly utters as she stares off into the middle space. How long was I sitting with my ass out?

Absorbing the tone shift, Carl visibly sees Jamie's newly formed fluster. "Something happen when I was out?" Carl asks.

"What's that?"

"You. You okay?"

"...I think I'm okay."

"It's a-okay if you're not a-okay, okay?" Carl's escalating concern is escorted by a soft smile. Humility has awarded Carl the ability to authentically discuss sensitive personal issues as if it were idle chitchat.

"I think so."

"Can you start a sentence without 'I think'?""I th—"

"Ewwwnnnn," Carl intervenes with that soft smile.

"—am doing well."

"Alright. Because you'd let me know."

"Yup. Of course."

"In person, CB, phone, carrier pigeon, whenever, whatever," Carl reassures her as he looks at the bill. "I got you on this."

"No, let me throw in."

"Get me next time."

It's futile to continue. Interactions like this have happened hundreds of times over thousands of miles. Their preferred form of currency is food. "Thank you."

"Anytime."

"Hey, um...have you ever...lost time." Learning from how she felt when she vindicated her mother, Jamie thinks that putting her troubles into words could kickstart their mend. And right this instant includes Carl's 'whenever, whatever.'

"Whattaya mean?"

"No memory of how you got places," Jamie sheepishly tells the table.

"Hell yeah, I zone the fuck out all the time. I don't know how get to half my destinations," Carl remarks as he puts money down on the table.

"I mean, like, not in the truck?

"When I drank myself stupid, I lost most days. Somethin' like that?"

"Not that either. Simple stuff. Not realizing the sun came up."

"Well, that's sleep." It starts as a joke but ends sincerely.

"...or going from one room to another."

"This new?"

"Yeah."

"It happen a lot," Carl's voice pitches, going from a baritone to a raspy tenor.

"It's starting to."

Carl drinks in the lack of eye contact. "...maybe you should call off the freight."

A lightning flash memory of herself in bed makes Jamie immediately respond. "No no, I'm good on this."

"Seriously, you're only a day out. Call Sally, tell her what's going on, and drive it back. I'll drive back with you."

"I can't do that to you. Come on."

"You'd do the same—you've done the same for me, so, yeah...what do you need?"

Jamie makes eye contact after avoiding it for far too long. "...I need to get going."

Jamie and Carl walk side by side toward their respective trucks. "Want some incense? I've got some incense?" Carl asks.

"I'm good. Thanks though."

"Sure? Your bunk can smell like a thunderstorm or a midnight full moon?" They stop near Carl's truck.

"That's right, you like smells that aren't really smells."

"Shit soothes the shit out of me. Plus, full moon I think," Carl points to the amorphous orb of pale light behind the clouds.

"Is it?"

"I don't know. Probably. It's bright."

"It is bright," Jamie remarks as they hug. Carl's torso feels as if he were hiding salad bowls under his shirt. His build causes Jamie to notice her gut graze his thighs. She can't recall if this was normal or just the result of their inverting bodies. "See you at Pitney?"

"Yeah, I'll be there. We can try out the weights."

"Oh man, yeah, but let me at least get a brisk walk in before I try, you know, health again."

"You'll be fine. Come here," the two hug again with a hearty pat on the back. "Alright-y, let me know if you need anything." Carl steps up and opens his driver's side door.

He uses the assistant step.

"Same here," Jamie adds.

"You got it," Carl says as he closes the door.

With her eyes on the ground and hands in her pockets, Jamie starts walking past Carl's truck. His engine starts and the exhaust blows a wisp of white feathers across her feet. When the red of Carl's taillights turn toward the back of Pic-A-Lili's,

Jamie uses the illumination to see the chicken coops. encased in shrubs and briars, the flimsy wooden coops are being inspected by the hefty chef of Pic-A-Lilli's. With a flashlight in hand, he surveys a splintered side of the shack furthest from the restaurant. A stiff breeze dusts up chicken feathers that not only get in his mouth, but ash his cheap cigar. He spits and coughs as he wipes his eyes with his stained shirt. Carl's light fades away as his truck enters the highway. Darkness returns to the coops. A sliver of light from the Chef's flashlight remains but and turns into her truck alleyway.

Between trailers, Jamie reaches for the handle of her truck.

"Excuse me," a thin female voice intrudes.

"Jesus!" Jamie turns to see the girl from the bar sitting against the end of her trailer.

The girl is seated on the ground by the driver's side tire of Jamie's truck. She slides her way up the truck to her feet. "Sorry, sorry, sorry."

"Why would you...ugh...scared me," Jamie pants.

"Yeah, yeah, sorry. I could have handled that better."

"Totally, yeah. Step out into the light so you're not a fucking spooky silhouette."

"Sure. Yeah, of course" the girls says as she steps out from the shadows and into the harsh tungsten light.

"So, hey, I'm Anita."

"Okay," Jamie coldly responds.

"And your name is?" Anita goes in for a handshake that Jamie wasn't expecting it.

"Oh, um, yeah," Jamie replies as she shakes her hand with as little contact as possible. "Jamie." An awkward greeting commences and the two follow up with an equally awkward silence.

"So, if you couldn't have guessed, I'm going to ask you—"

"For a ride; yeah, I figured."

Anita does an animated point with a desperately optimistic flare. "Exactly. Yes! A ride is the prize I seek."

"Sorry, but I made it a habit to not pick up any more hitchhikers," Jamie half-heartedly mumbles.

"Ah, but you went with 'any more' , meaning you at one time did."

If you could kill a person with a mere glower, Anita would be on the ground. "...okay," Jamie responds after an earth-stopping pause.

"So, you at least had one hitchhiker."

"Yup."

"Meaning that it's in your realm of possibilities."

"I see where you're going with this, but I've been burnt too many times."

"Ah, okay, I get it, but that doesn't have to be us. I once knew this married couple that met from hitchhiking."

"I doubt this is our meet cute."

"Well, a good meet cute is rocky at first and in my humble opin—"

"Where are you heading anyway?" Jamie interrupts.

"North."

"See, I'm heading South, so sorry."

"Hm, right on, well...," Anita's lips tighten as she performs a series of defeated nods. "Thanks anyway."

"See you around," Jamie says to Anita's exit.

"Probably."

Jamie watches Anita vanish around the corner of her truck. She remains gawking at nothing and replays the odd interaction in her head. After a moment, Jamie shakes it off and uses the assistant step without a shred of guilt.

———

Jamie downshifts at the exit ramp to head north. She looks to the passenger's side rearview mirror. Anita smokes a cigarette outside of Pic-A-Lilli's. Her feet are on the seat of the bench while she sits on its back. Goddamn it. How? Wherever she sits turns into an Edward Hopper painting. Jamie grabs her thermos and takes a ship. Anita's still there, so a decision has been made. "Ugh," Jamie utters as she dramatically cuts the wheel and turns south, away from her destination.

As the glow of the Pic-A-Lilli's neon dissipates, Jamie nods with relief. Feeling distant enough from the restaurant, and

her social anxieties, she begins to turn around. Circumnav-
igating that awkward scenario is so elating, Jamie smiles to
herself by herself. She turns the wheel and cuts through the
vacant intersection.

"'At least one hitchhiker.'" Jamie sees Pic-A-Lilli's in the
distance and accelerates, spying outside the approaching tavern. Anita is nowhere to be seen. "'It's in your realm of possibilities.'" Shamelessly, Jamie and her truck pass Pic-A-Lilli's.
"'I knew a married couple,' yeah, well, bet they're divorced."

Jamie listens to the radio as she drives into the night. She
originally turned it on to distract her brain from reciting every interaction from the tavern. Success. She's now synched
into a flow state and her synapses are content with their placid
duties. She doesn't even know the radio is on until it starts to
waver in and out of silence. The lights on the radio join its
fading sound and the headlights dim. "Oh god, what?" The
dashboard lights flicker away to nothing, and her gas pedal
suddenly becomes inert. "What? No, no, no, no, no, no, how?
How?" An empty gas tank illuminates on the dashboard.
"There's no way. That's not a thing. That's not a thing that's
happening! There's no way!"

Jamie starts cutting the wheel, but it gets more and
more labor-intensive with each cut. "Jeeeeezus, that's heavy.
Thaaaaaaaat's heavy!" Jamie's truck gets to the side of the road
just before the engine putters to an end. "Son of a shit!" Jamie
exclaims as she jerks into a stop. "Ugh...okay," Jamie tells her
steering wheel as she buries her face into it. "Keep it together.
Keep it together. And one last time, keep it together."

A flippant hand, without the assistance of eyes, reaches for
CB receiver. There are a few flailing misses but she eventually
grips the radio.

"Gamey Jamie to Dispatch," Jamie says with her face
pressed against the wheel.

"Go for Dispatch," a clear male voice answers.

Jamie looks into the driver's side mirror. There's just road
and nothingness behind her. As the residual adrenaline courses through her body, it mixes with the success of the Pic-A-Lilli's venture. "You know what, Dispatch, false alarm."

"10-4, Gamey Jamie."

"Thank you, over," Jamie hangs up her radio and opens the door. She takes a deep breath to reinforce her uptick in mood. Before she exits, she grabs her thermos, takes a pill from her prescription bottle and knocks it back. "Alright, brisk walk." Jamie steps out. Her ego gets an extra boost from slamming the door that holds the neglected logbook.

Jamie ties a white rag to her door handle. The distance between streetlights seems to lengthen the further down the road they go. If her pre-excursion ritual works for the tires under her feet, why not just her feet? Jamie rolls her neck and gyrates her hips. "Hey, hey, look at that. No cracking sou-AGH!" Jamie blurts when her left shoulder cracks while limbering up. "Well, okay then, here we go." She stands in the middle of the road and turns her back to the moonlight. She takes a deep breath followed by a twice as long exhale. After four steps, Jamie mumbles "Oh, boy."

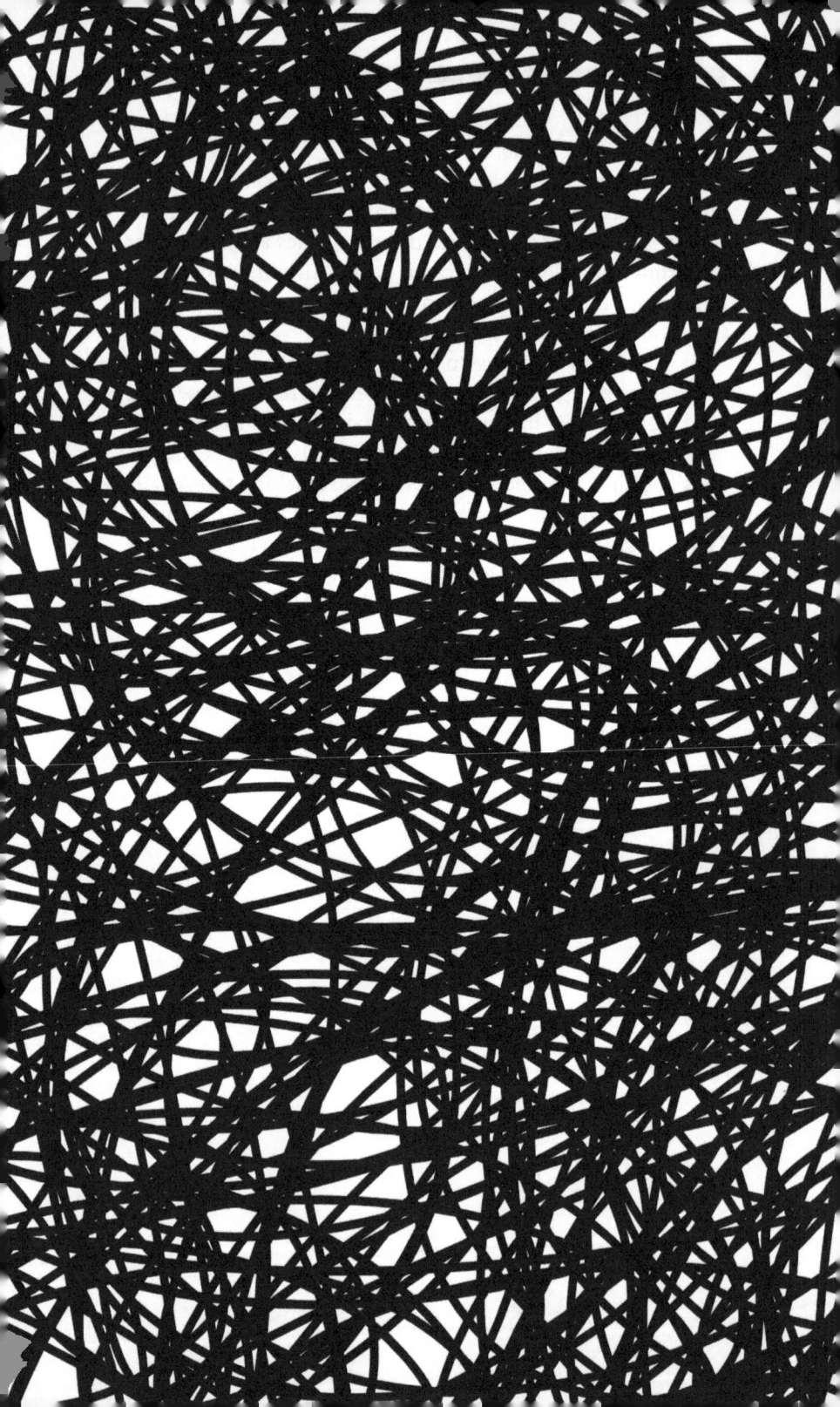

4

SAUNTERING FOR AT LEAST AN HOUR, JAMIE DID NOT FEEL LIKE she's actually moved. The visage of the road in front of her stays the same, but her truck is no longer behind her. A comfortable wave of vertigo blankets Jamie. She can't remember the last time she had this much free space in front or behind her. The moonlit cumulus clouds made the mystifying expanse of the night sky tangible. As if she could grab it. The moon finally makes an appearance. Not quite full but shining as if it is, the celestial body shines between magenta clouds.

She looks down from the heavens and sees that the moon is bright enough to cast a shadow. Extending her hand, she can make a lunar shadow on the pavement. She fiddles her digits, waving a silhouette over the pale blue concrete. Then nothing. The shadow joins the darkness. Jamie looks up.

Billowing with life, the clouds pass by the luminous moon. Her eyes descend back to the street. The visibility of the forest waxes at the whims of the sky. Bubbles of gentle illumination dance through the greenery, like spotlights waggling over an audience. It's thick and coarse. Bark and shrubs make up the majority of its body.

A rustle can be heard from the woods. Jamie turns. It's not abrupt or loud enough to cause alarm, but it does warrant her attention. Atop a mound, in a small clearing of thicket, a deer looks at Jamie from a distance. It's a mere silhouette, but its eyes reflect a piercing gaze. It's hard to comprehend why, but the deer's dimensions seem skewed. Its neck looks stouter yet its limbs seem longer than the average deer's. The antlers give Jamie a faint flutter of relief. Short, rounded and covered in velvet, Jamie can't remember the term but knows this is a "teenage" buck.

The clouds, once again, cover the moon. Right before the light leaves the deer's position, the animal initiates standing upright. It doesn't rear onto its back legs. It stands. Its posture adjusts as its shoulders arch and its head tilts forward. It keeps its glare on Jamie right before it's swallowed by darkness.

"Uhhhhh...uhhhhh...," Jamie moans. She checks to see if she was mistaken. Maybe her truck is obscured by some greenery, and it is in walking, possibly running, distance. To her dismay, her truck is nowhere in her line of sight, but a second wave of moonlight is.

Jamie looks toward the deer. In the distance, four more standing deer stare at Jamie. Shrouded by the night, all Jamie can see are eyes and shapes. They're slightly different in stature but all a part of the same "species". However, the other three have hardened and sharpened antlers affixed to their humanoid skulls.

"Hey! Hey!" Jamie Hollers in an attempt to scare them off. " Back...BACK! Don't you—FUCK!" Once again invisible from cloud coverage, the moon light almost instantaneously returns. What was four is now nine. The lurking creatures come in varying sizes. Some stand near the height of treetops while others are no more than four feet tall. With just a glimpse of their long limbs and striking eyes, Jamie's breath exits her lungs. They're walking. They're walking toward Jamie.

"Ahhhh—SHIT! HOLY SHIT!" Struck down by fright, Jamie sprints away. Unaware of direction, Jamie barrels down the highway, away from her truck.

"Holy shit! Holy fucking shit! Holy mother of shit!" Out of breath, she turns to look behind her. Her hopes to slow down her sprint to a march are dashed away. "Shit, shit, shit, shit..." she yelps between pants. The shadowed beasts step out of the brush and peer toward Jamie. "SHIT! Monsters! Deer monsters!" Jamie overrides her burning legs and hammering heart. She maintains her sprint and stays onward as long as her body will let her.

Having an end in sight, Jamie decelerates at the sight of salvation. Pic-A-Lilli's hideous neon is now a beacon to sanctuary. She stops for a moment, heaves forward and hacks up a fistful of saliva. Concerning, considering she assumed she was just going to cough. Fear forces its hand as her hand flicks away the spit. Her lungs feel hot and acidic. As if they are lined with rust. Also concerning considering you shouldn't be able to "feel" your lungs. A problem for a later time. She must sally forth, but at the rhythm of hyperventilation. The parking lot is absent of trucks and only a few motorcycles pepper the exterior.

One last look before she re-enters the dive of dives. Nothing is stalking her or at least she can't see anything stalking her. "Okay, okay, okay, okay. No more deer monsters. No more of that," she pants as she punches her knuckles together. As she makes her way into Pic-A-Lilli's a thought crosses her mind. *Huh.* That's been the longest she's gone without self-flagellation for quite some time. A triumph considering the instigators.

Not quite as bustling as the last time she visited, Jamie lurches inside. With a labored breath, she feels muscles she forgot she had seize up on her. Jamie leans against the desolate bar. Lou, the bartender with rolled-up sleeves, hair the color of concrete and a face etched from it, steps in front of Jamie. A cherry stem takes the place of a toothpick in Lou's mouth. He patiently awaits Jamie's order.

"Mmmmm, uh ah. Oh god," Jamie pants. "Just ah, just give me a...oh god...," Jamie catches her breath as her head dangles toward the floor.

"You're good," Lou answers as he pours her a glass of water.

"Okay, here we go," Jamie says in her first complete sentence since the deer incident. She sits on her stool and collects her composure. Hands are folded and phlegm is swallowed before a proper "Hello."

"'lo Jamie," Lou greets with stoic eyes.

In one action, Jamie finishes Lou's eight-ounce glass of water. Clinking it back to the bar, as if she were in a saloon, she perks back up. "Yeah, yeah, um....St—" Jamie can't remember ever seeing this bartender, let alone meeting him.

"Lou," he intercepts Jamie's blind guess of "Steve"."That's right, Lou," Jamie fibs. "Hey, Lou."

"Hey," Lou nods and then continues the transaction, acknowledging Jamie's rattled constitution. "What can I get you?"

"Uh, a shot of something."

"What kind of something?'

"I don't know."

"Gotcha." Lou then abruptly walks off.

"Wait, um, I—okay" Jamie watches Lou walk away and in craning her neck discovers Anita sitting on the other end of the bar. "Oh no, wow," Jamie whispers with eye contact and a false smile.

Anita timidly waves to Jamie and Jamie returns the gesture with a fragile wrist. Jamie's smile comes along with an ignominious hiss through her teeth. Anita gets up. "Oh god, no," Jamie continues to sputter. "Please don't—Hey," Jamie remarks, shifting her tone as Anita confidently strides into her proximity.

"What's happening, Jamie?" Anita asks with a drop in her hip and a click on her heels.

I know that's supposed to be cute, but Nazi stormtroopers did that. "Anita, how are you?" Jamie asks in a stilted cadence.

"Minimal shab in my direction. Still schlepping about" Anita says as she sits down next to Jamie.

"Ah 'Minimal shab'," Jamie repeats.

"You? What brought you back here?"

"Eh. My truck—" Lou puts a shot down in front of Jamie. "Thank you," Jamie says as she picks up the shot glass.

"Yup," Lou responds.

"Hey, what is—" Lou is gone on to other patrons before Jamie finishes her question. "My truck ran out of gas," Jamie reveals as she takes the shot. "Eh, that was either terrible gin or decent vodka," she cringes before she clinks it onto the graffiti-riddled bar.

"You ran out of gas?" Anita asks as she motions to Lou for one of the terrible gins or decent vodkas.

"Mmm hmm."

"I thought semis had massive gas tanks?"

"They sure do, 100-gallon tank." Seeing Lou amble their way, Jamie motions the glass to him. "Another of whatever the hell this was, please." Lou nods.

"Wow, how'd you miss that?" Anita asks.

"Two of them. I missed two 100-gallon tanks."

"Sheesh."

"I'm hoping someone siphoned my gas while I was here."

"Why would you hope that?"

"It's either that, or I'm a cocktail of psychotic and incompetent."

"Psychompetent."

"I can manage one but both?"

Lou pours the shot from a "white-lightning" whiskey jug. He caps it and puts it back under the bar. For a sturdy man, it takes Lou some effort to hoist the jug back into its resting place.

"Jesus, moonshine," Jamie says as she watches Lou approach.

"Handwritten label," Anita adds.

Lou places the two glasses in front of Anita and Jamie. Anita lifts the spirit with an aim to cheers, but Jamie takes the shot of irony.

"Agh, jeeezus," Jamie cringes with one eye closed.

"It's more for the fucking-up than the flavor," Anita remarks while drinking hers as if it were sugar. There's little reaction to the potency from Anita, but Jamie takes notice.

Jamie rolls her eyes at Anita's pain tolerance. "Must have been this brand's motto." Jamie clinks the glass down again and directs her attention back to Lou. "What do I owe you?"

"Sixteen," Lou responds while picking up the glass and wiping the bar.

Jamie's casually reaches for her wallet, but the action quickly becomes manic. "Oh, fuck, come on. No..."

Miles away from Pic-A-Lili's, through potential cryptozoo-logical terrain, Jamie's wallet rests comfortably on her truck's dashboard.

"What's up?" Anita asks an alarmed Jamie.

"My wallet."

"What about it?"

"How did I forget my fucking wallet?"

"How did you forget your wallet?"

"I'm frazzled and stressed and psycho-something-or-other."Psychompetent."

"That's it."

"I can get this round," says Anita as she places her back-pack on her lap.

Jamie halts in her search and faces Anita. "Oh, thanks but I'm—"

"What? You're going to walk back to your truck, which is probably like...milesssss?"

Jamie reluctantly nods. "A few, yes."

"—and then walk alllllll the way back here." Anita mim-ics Jamie by having her index and middle fingers walk to and from the bar on the bar.

"I-uh-I guess."

"Nonsense, I got you."

"Really, it's fine."

"Nonsense, you're spewing nonsense" Anita takes out her wallet from her backpack. Jamie's sly eye attempts to get a peek inside her bag but only fabric and hands are caught. "Bam!" Anita exclaims as she places thirty dollars on the counter. She grips her ratty wallet with both hands and shovels it back deep into her bag.

"Um, thank you."

"No, problem-o."

"That really saved me."

"What about gas?"

"Oh, no no, that's too much."

"Doubling downon the nonsense, huh?"

"It's not that crazy of a walk to the nearest gas station," Jamie tells herself along with Anita.

"I don't know, walking back to your truck, grabbing your wallet, then walking back this way past this lovely delicatessen." Anita gleefully nods at Lou. He points to her with a raised brow as if she had a request. "Oh no, we're good, sorry," Anita apologizes and returns to her rant. "Getting gas and walking alllllllllll the way back to your truck while lugging gas?"

"Most plans sound bad when you, you know...explain them...out loud."

"We could take turns carrying the gas can."

"Ah," Jamie interjects. *I knew it. This level of charm is not sustainable.*

"Yup."

"So, it's for a ride?"

"Hell yeah, it's for a ride. I'm a wayward vagabond, with only adventure as a destination. I'm not handing out handouts." The shot of moonshine aids that manifesto.

"Ugh, I don't know."

"Plus, do you really want to take that spooky walk back by yourself?"

Antlers. Jamie stares at Anita with a tense brow and wrinkled lips. *Antlers.* The two shots lend a hand in her decision—*Antlers*—but a companion, or a sacrifice, during a potential deer monster attack is appealing.

Just as they pass Pic-A-Lilli's, the strength of Jamie's grip couldn't carry Styrofoam. The strain, compounded with the tension of wondering what's behind every rustle in the woods, breaks Jamie's stride. "Hey, do you, um—" Jamie babbles.

"Want me to take a go?" Anita finishes Jamie's thought.

"If you don't mind."

"Gimmie here," Anita proposes.

"Thank you," Jamie says as she steps away from the metal diesel gas can. Before Anita lifts the container off the ground, she catches the frantic anxiety in Jamie's eyes. The gauzy clouds move on and the moon hides behind the trees. Without that celestial glow, the night loses its mysticism.

"And here we go." Anita lifts the petrol and the two continue onward. Anita's shimmying is just a touch faster than Jamie's median walking speed. So, the added weight slows Anita to Jamie's pace.

At this speed of trudge, Anita can only take silence for so long. "So is it, like, hubris or something?"

"What's that?" Jamie asks, fixated on everything besides Anita.

"Well, earlier, you told me I couldn't get a ride because I was going north and you were going south, but here we are walking... North."

"Uh—" Jamie's fixation on the woods finds Anita.

"And you'd know I'd know that, right? We're not going to forget that interaction, but, you know, here we are."

"I uh...uhhhhh..."

"There is an easy out. You can just nod or something and we can both forget this happened in four minutes and start talking about cool shit like panini presses and contact juggling. I'd rather do that than be uncomfortably silent for hours because you don't want to be uncomfortable for four seconds."

It's an impressive feat to take the attention away from what may lurk in the dark.

"Is contact juggling with the glass ball and you kind of—" Jamie mocks the gesture of contact juggling.

"Yes! Oh, man, you want to try? I got mine with me."

"Oh, jeeze, god no," Jamie retorts.

"Sure? Just in my bag?"

"No thanks, it seems like you have to defy psychics," is a sentence that resonates. Jamie all but categorizes the "deer incident" as a momentary lapse in sanity. Maybe influenced by the spooky surroundings and distressing circumstances.

"I know, right?"

Jamie naturally gravitates in step with Anita's ambulate. The rest of the walk is wrought with frivolous chitchat and that is an equal preference for both parties.

With zero dramatic turns, the driver's side door opens. "Oh, thank god," says Jamie at the sight of her wallet. There's a faint memory of flopping her wallet on the dashboard while she was intoxicated by the compounding frustrations that accompany vanishing petrol..

"It there?" Anita asks, still on the street.

"Sure is." Jamie adds, crawling into the front seat. She grabs her wallet and slides back down as if her truck were a terrible kindergarten slide.

"Good. Great news. Great."

Flustered by counting money, Jamie gives up and just hands Anita every bill in her wallet.

"Oh, I'm all good. Thank you though." Anita waves off the courtesy. Distracted by the truck itself, Anita takes off her hat to get the entirety of the vehicle in her vision.

"Come on. You helped me out way more than you had to."

"I'm good, really, I'm just happy for the company. And the ride. Pay it back by paying it forward." With her gaze glued to the truck, Anita pantomimes "stepping back to step forward" to further express her proposal.

Quietly humbled by the gesture, Jamie puts her money back in her wallet and almost tosses it back into the truck. Her better judgment crams it into her inside jacket pocket.

"Ok then, thank you. That's um...thank you."

"My pleasure," Anita says as she studies the back of the trailer.

Heaving the gas can off the ground, Jamie dumps the nozzle into the metallic barrel.

"Don't you have to get to the engine and light a match or something?" Anita asks after a quick peek.

"My old rig did. This guy's pretty self-managing" Jamie remarks as she continues to gush gasoline.

"Ah, old truck. Been a trucker a while?"

"Right after I graduated Dean's List for my Bachelor in Fine Arts." Jamie thought the sentence's latent sarcasm was strong enough to warrant her believable delivery.

"You went to art school?"

"Thought about it," Jamie says as she slaps the cap back onto the gas can "Ready?" Jamie says to Anita, vanishing behind the truck.

"Shoulda went."

Not wanting to interrupt, but anxious to continue, Jamie interjects Anita's moment at the best of her ability. "So, um, what's you doing?"

"Just drinking in your truck here."

"Pretty standard model, really."

"Well, it's yours, making it the only one like it."

"Then all trucks are unique, making them not."

"All the same, different perspective."

"Well, I'm getting in. Meet you on the other side." There's a brief moment where Jamie is left to herself. Inside her truck and behind the wheel, Jamie gets a second to calculate a scenario. Part of her hope is Anita doesn't show up on the passenger's side. That, somehow, Anita was a figment of Jamie's imagination. Not a healthy thought, but it would carry over credence to the deer creatures she saw earlier. If that is the case, and the more bizarre facets of the day are the result of a defective pathology, she would at least know she's insane.

*Can you know you're crazy? "I think therefore I am?" Isn't that a thing? Does that apply to what I'm thinking? I can't be crazy 'cause I'm askin' if I'm crazy? There's a trickster demon or something? I think that might only be if I exist? Like I have to exist because something has to ask if I exist? I still don't know why a nonexistent thing can't have that thought—oh, fuck she's real—*Jamie's thoughts are cut short by an opening truck door.

"Whoa, ho." Anita says as she plops down on the passenger's seat. "Damn, that step's helpful for getting up in here."

"Welcome, I guess."

"I have to say, it's pretty swanky in here," Anita comments with wondering eyes.

"Really? I mean, it's clean." *She on shrooms?*

"Clean can be swanky," Anita says while petting the dashboard.

"I guess. I think I just don't have that much stuff." *Pills?*

"Minimalism! I like it. It's a thing and I like it."

"It's not on purpose. You should see my apartment," Jamie shifts the car into neutral and keeps the key cranked.

"What's going on here?"

"Priming it, so I can do this," Jamie says as she shifts into park and cranks the key one more time. The truck pops like a firecracker and an aggressive grumble follows. Anita can feel her hand vibrate on the dashboard. Jamie presses down on the gas. The truck roars to life and that grumble reaches a steady and confident tempo. The obedience of the wheel returns to Jamie's hands.

"Ah, that must feel good to hear," Anita comments.

"It's not bad," Jamie says as she cuts the wheel.

Maybe pills.

As Jamie shifts, she gets lost in the image of Anita in the passenger's seat. Starring in the middle space between her clavicle and the passenger's window, Jamie freezes in the moment.

"You okay?" Anita asks.

Jamie's gaze returns to the immediate and she eases on the clutch. "Yeah, sorry. Just been a minute since someone sat in that seat."

"I'm glad I can give it back its purpose."

"...okay."

Yeah, pills.

———

Gaining some momentum from the side of the road, the truck merges onto the vacant highway.

Bathed in bleak halogen, Jamie leans against her vehicle with her back to a grim gas station. A convenience booth sits under a putrid yellow streetlight and Jamie finds Anita buying something from the cashier. He's doing his best to pretend he wasn't sleeping. He even waits for Anita to exit through the glass door to rest his head back on the counter.

"Jerky?" Anita asks with a fresh plastic bag drooping from her wrist.

"I'm okay," Jamie responds. Jamie's pass stuns Anita. "... huh" she coos as she walks back off toward her seat.

Slightly offended by the *she think I can't turn down food?* Jamie puts the nozzle back into the pump and climbs into her seat.

Anita's already eating the jerky by the time Jamie takes her seat. As she sinks into her chair, Jamie's eyes are thrown a distraction. "What's that?

A tiny toy skeleton, playing an accordion, is suction-cupped to the dashboard. Judging from its off-white bone color and era of popularity, this thing is thirty to forty years old.

"Well, I didn't name him yet, but I was thinking of going with something like Skull McCartney. It could also be a girl, so if we ignore the lack of rib, Skulla Abdul."

Jamie, not incredibly enthused about her new dashboard ornament, grits through her displeasure. "I wouldn't say no to Skulla Deen."

"She couldn't play the accordion."

"Could Paula Abdul?"

"I'm not sure if McCartney did, but I bet he could figure it out."

With a rotation of the neck, Jamie shifts. "McCartney it is." She takes her thermos, but after a quick glance at Anita, stops unscrewing the lid. She conceals the thermos on the side of her seat, furthest away from Anita. It doesn't quite fit, so she crams her thermos into the compartment built into the door. It'll only fit if Jamie crumples the logbook and she doesn't hesitate. They then exit the gas station and continue their journey north. Skull McCartney gently bobbles as they drive.

"Come on, you turn down jerky, but not a single qualm with Spam," Anita reads off the side of a discovered can of cheap meat.

"I used to eat jerky all the time. I needed to change it up."

"I get it, but when it comes to all the affordable-pre-cooked-canned-meats in the world?"

"It's the champagne of affordable precooked-canned-meats."

"Pork with ham." Those're the ingredients. It's like saying cow with beef."

"How's that different from sausage?"

"It comes out of a can with a little key, that's how."

"Off the grill with a fried egg and a warm biscuit. It's a sandwich that's hard to beat. Kimmy loved them," Jamie reveals.

Anita winces a bit before she answers. "Ooo, fried egg, and a new name...Kimmy?"

Jamie's eyes twitch from the slip of the tongue "Kimberly, yeah, um, my daughter."

"Aw hell, I didn't know. That's cool. How old?"

"Seven, no six—wait, no, no seven."

"Right on. That's a good time, seven. Who has a bad memory from Seven?"

"Well, she can probably name a few," Jamie says to the open road.

"Sorry, I didn't mean to breach into private stuff."

"It just stings a bit."

"We can drop it. I missed the past tense there."

"It's okay. She's didn't die or anything."

"Oh, thank God."

"There was just a nasty divorce."

"Oof, sorry."

"One thing for adults to go through litigation, but a kid...?"

"Went that far, huh?"

"Unfortunately. You want to see her?"

"Of course." Anita accepts this with an emphatic smile and all of her attention.

Jamie flips over the visor and cautiously removes the ripped photo. Jamie hands the photo over to an equally cautious Anita. A pang of reluctant appreciation plucks Jamie's spirit. *At least she knows when to dial back that grade-school art-teacher wonderment.*

"Look at that. Beautiful girl. That's a memory-making photo of you two."

" 'You two?'" Jamie's questions with a glance at the photo. Anita displays it before she hands it back. Jamie is now in the photo, smiling behind Kimberly. Before Kimberly was alone on the park bench, now she is on the lap of a cheerful mother. The tear goes through Jamie instead of Kimberly.

"...um, ah," Jaimie putters as she takes her pharmacy-printed memory. A second look and a second guess of reality is needed before she puts it back.

"There a story behind that photo?" Anita asks.

"Um, yeah...uh...," Jamie excavates the memories from her mental fog.

"It must be rough, with your schedule and getting the time to see her and whatnot?"

"Yeah, that was kind of it, right? In the summer, she'd have off of school and she just got big enough to not need a car seat. We experimented with taking her on routes. Make it like a mom and daughter trip, try to hit museums and landmarks and such," Jamie reveals.

"Looked fun."

"It actually was. I was afraid she'd be bored, but she liked seeing new places and screwing around on the CB. Colored a lot. Lots of coloring. The trip was never really that long, anyway. Little over a week."

"Kids can do a little over a week," Anita adds.

"Yeah. It was better than her sticking around the house all day or finding a day care when her dad was at work."

"Another one in the future? I mean, if you can?"

"Um, the pipe dream was to make it a tradition, you know? Every summer a trip or two? Bond and whatnot. But I don't think that's a thing now," Jamie stammers.

"Why the hell not?" Anita asks with a dash of aggravation.

Startled by Anita's concern, Jamie makes brief eye contact to see its authenticity. Anita's lips are furled and brow tensed. It's somehow seems genuine. "It's ah...it doesn't look likely."

"Oh, come on, you two want it, you should get it" Anita says.

"My ex actually has sole custody and we're not on the best of terms, so um, that part gets kind of rough."

"Whoa, sorry," Anita remarks after a sigh. She tamps down her frustrations and directs her eyes outside of her window.

"Yeah, that's been a...hurdle." Just saying it softens the pinch of the circumstances.

"I bet she still wants to see you as much as possible though."

"I don't know. It's been just as taxing on her than it has been on us."

"Yeah, it would have to be."

"And I don't want to make it worse, you know?"

"Of course."

"It's actually my fault. The whole thing is my fault. Getting past that has been...not a breeze."

"You probably won't," Anita throws away with the same warmth as her previous sentiments. Jamie's eyes replace the road with Anita's. "That sounds like something you're just going to have to learn to manage."

"Ugh." Jamie's amygdala stabs at every avenue for a decent rebuttal, but even a twenty-something hippy type can acknowledge a sobering truth.

"Believe me," Anita's tone shifts.

"Yeah?" Jamie downshifts her emotions along with her gear to a steady cruising speed. Eight miles per hour above the speed limit. Faster than the legal speed but not fast enough to be illegal. The conversation hits a pleasant groove that they both would consider "real." If they continue, there's a high likelihood that the chat of becoming "profound." "My life's a cavalcade of fucking up. Why do you think I'm—Holy Shit! Look out" Anita screams. Jamie darts her eyes to the road, but it's too late. She captures a glimpse of a limping man and plows over him with all seventy-three-thousand pounds of semi-trailer. A thud thunders throughout the truck. Loud, but Jamie could barely feel the impact under the weight of the truck. Jamie shifts and slams on the brakes. That, she can feel. Steam billows from the screeching tires and Jamie winces as she pumps the brakes. Adrenaline courses as she somehow tries not to destroy the truck that destroyed a man. The trailer pivots as the chassis of the truck grinds down the road. Yanking the wheel side to side, the trailer is saved from going perpendicular in the middle of a highway. Still a tad askew, the truck stops, taking up both lanes. Skull McCartney continues to thrash as the two passengers stay tense.

Panting into her wheel, Jamie unbuckles her seatbelt and lifts her head. She can feel a bruise from the seatbelt start to form across her chest.

"Billy?" Jamie questions toward the windshield.

"What?" An alarmed and braced Anita squeaks.

"Um, you okay? You alright?" Jamie asks.

"Yeah, yeah, I think so," the jittering head of Anita answers.

"Okay," Jamie says looking to the now stagnant Skull Mc-Cartney. She only got a fraction of a second glimpse of whom she ran down. Jamie looks into her rearview mirror to see if there is a mangled trail of Billy's remains. Nothing. The clutch sticks after such a harsh maneuver, but Jamie is able to roll the truck to the side of the road.

"Oh god, oh god, oh god," Jamie repeats as the truck parks.

Jamie steps out and cold air jabs her hot face. It's in the distance. The sight of it causes her heart to pound in her ears. Something that may not even be a man rushes into the darkness of the woods. A mere shadow, it didn't appear injured, but most importantly, appeared alive. Anita asks a question, but all Jamie can hear is muffled murmuring.

"What? Billy!" Jamie barks. Jogging to the end of her trailer. "Was that you? Billy!" Jamie hollers into the woods.

Anita steps out of the truck. "Jamie? Hey."

"Do you see anything?" Jamie asks the approaching Anita.

"No, I think it ran back into the woods."

Failing to hear or see a response from the thick darkness, Jamie marches to the front of the truck. "Holy shit, this is bad."

"What do we do?" Anita asks as she trails behind.

"Ah, fuck me," Jamie says at a large dent, accompanied by a smattering of blood, on the reflective grill of the truck. "Ugh, we have to call the police."

Anita slinks up behind her. "For a deer? That seems extreme."

"Deer? A person. I hit a person."

"I get that you think that with whoever Billy is, but that was a deer."

"No. No, no, no, no, no, no. Person. That was a man. That was—" Jamie realizes the odds of Billy being in this location, on foot, at this time exact time. Then she projects attempting to try and explain that to Anita."...um, a deer?"

"Yeah, check it out." Anita grabs a clump of red slick fur from the grill of the truck. She lowers it into headlights. Jamie, dumfounded, gently opens her palm to the remains. Anita places the pelt into Jamie's hand as hers is placed on Jamie's shoulder.

"Yes, you didn't kill anybody. In fact, I don't think you killed a deer."

Jamie investigates the patch of animal fur in her hand and looks to the road. There isn't even a streak of gore on the asphalt. "Okay...okay. That was, um, that was scary."

"You know what? Why don't we call it a night. Truckers sleep, right? You should sleep."

"I'm not good with sleep."

"Still need it."

"You can't be around me when I'm asleep."

Confused, Anita suppresses some frustration before she answers. "Okay, creepy line to throw out at any time, let alone in the middle of the night in the middle of nowhere but...," Anita takes the bloodied scalp from Jamie's palm and tosses it into the brush. "Fair enough. You should sleep, anyhow. I bet you're past due," Anita declares as she wipes her hands on her pants.

Anita politely shuttles Jamie to the driver's side of the truck.

"Yeah, you're right. It'd do me well."

"Right? We'll worry about making up for lost time in the morning."

"Sounds good."

"How do we do that? You have to get to a rest stop or something, yeah?

"There's one less than ten miles from here."

"Right on. You going to make it?"

"I think—yeah, yeah I got this" Jamie inclines, remembering her interaction with Carl.

Anita opens the driver's side door. She watches Jamie crawl into the driver's seat. "I have a little bit of experience with 18-wheelers if you need me to drive."

"Really?"

"Hitchhiker, right? I'm sure you could talk me through it."

"I'm good, really, but thanks. And seriously, we have to figure out the sleeping situation. You can't be near me," Jamie says while looking down at Anita from the perch of her seat.

"Why? You like a sleep-induced werewolf? REM bring out the vampire?"

"Close. Mental disorder," Jamie closes the door to a dumbstruck Anita.

Anita walks back around to her side and notices her shadow projecting on the white of the trailer. She does a quick doubletake for her luna-eclipsed silhouette. She trills her fingers in the moonlight before she heads to the passenger's side door.

5

"MUM...MUM...MUM MUM MUM." A HUSHED JUVENILE VOICE NUDGES.

"Mm, ehhh," Jamie expels through a closed mouth. Her eyes flutter open to a delicate child. "Kimmy..."

"Can I feed Bob?" A bright-faced and brighter-haired Kimberly asks.

Jamie's eye widen as she props up her head. "Kimberly?" Jamie asks in her apartment's bedroom.

"He's hungry."

Jamie explodes into an upright position and presses herself against the wall beside her bed. "Kimberly."

Kimberly hops onto the bed and rolls onto her back to better flick her mother's knees. "He's asleep now, but he's hungry sleeping. Bob wants some breakfast."

Jamie, silent, looks around the room. It's no longer a shrine to depression, but a motherly furnished bedroom. There are no piles of mail, legal documents or liquor bottles in sight. There's only one child in Hawaiian pajamas in the bedroom of a semi-healthy person. Jamie's eyes lose focus as she collects her composure. A familiar object sharpens her vision. "Um...," Skull McCartney sits on a bedside table as his head gently bobbles with an expanded accordion.

"Why are you...? My truck somewhere?"

"Did you sleep in your clothes? Can I sleep in my clothes?" Kimberly ignores her mother's bafflement and rolls back over to her stomach.

Jamie looks down on herself. It's difficult to cerebrally navigate, but she thinks she's wearing the same outfit from the truck. In a dash of scrutiny, she whiffs her armpits. They're musty. As if she's been driving 16-plus hours on 3600 calories of roadside cuisine and sprinting away from ravenous deer mutants.

"And Bob, we should feed Bob," Kimberly reiterates. Jamie turns to a seemingly innocent Kimberly. She sits up into her lap, kicking her heels against the mattress.

Drinking in the moment, Jamie tenderly grips onto Kimberly's shoulders and hugs her in astonishment. "Yeah yeah,... sure thing, babe. Let's go feed Bob."

Bob is a lumpy slumbering mass of an English Bulldog. He's snoring while his head dangles off the well-used couch.

Jamie kneels down by the sink and Kimberly holds a bowl by Jamie's head. "Back up just a tad." Jamie opens the door to a plethora of dog food inside a plastic tub.

With a smirk and a quick fist pump, Jamie lightly exclaims "Alright, still there." Kimberly shuffles away as Jamie scoops up some dog food. "Ready?"

"Ready!"

Jamie pours the food into Kimberly's bowl. Joy continues to eagerly ram the doors to Jamie's caution. Relishing the nostalgia, she feels like she's flexing long-forgotten muscles. Emotions activate that she thought were dead and buried in her psyche.

"Um...be gentle when you wake him up."

"Okay-dokey," Kimberly says as she scampers away, spilling some kibble.

Awestruck. Jamie stands straight up. She scours her well-kept apartment as Kimberly crouches down to Bob's face. Gripping a few pieces of kibble, Kimberly crawls as if she were under adorable barbed wire, on the way to complete her bulldog mission. The uneven bowl of food stays on the floor in the kitchen.

"Bob. BoooOOOoooooOOb," Bob stays limp, but his eyes open to the sounds of a grumble and a snort. "Hungry hungry, Bob." Bob's tongue slurps out of his massive head and finds the kibble in Kimberly's tiny hand. "Eeeeeee!" Kimberly squeaks in laughter. Kimberly pats Bob's ample torso as he slinks and groans his way off the couch.

Jamie opens the fridge to find a couple of cans of Spam next to some actual food.

"Heh." An idea springs to Jamie so she opens the egg compartment. Half the eggs are cracked and hollow, but the other half are ready for breakfast sandwiches. Reaching for a bag of biscuits on top of the fridge, Jamie collects the ingredients on the counter. Lastly, the coup de grâce. Jamie snickers at the existence of the can of Spam in her hand.

Kimberly keeps shimmering back and forth from Bob and his bowl. She has created an edible trail for him to follow to his diminishing bowl. Each grab is met with a giggle and each drop is met with a giggle. Bob's lackadaisical temperament, and general fondness for his bipedal sister, allows Kimberly to follow through with her scheme.

Still transfixed by the can of processed pig parts, Jamie becomes overwhelmed by the sound of Kimberly's laughter.

"Kimmy, baby. What year is it?" Jamie asks with her eyes on the ample ingredient list.

When Kimberly stands up from Bob's bowl, she sees the can of Spam. With Spam in hand, Jamie shuffles over to the front door. Her markerboard calendar is still over the key rings. Instead of being spitefully scrawled over, the days are intact and filled with colorful notes. Unfortunately, the year was common knowledge when Jamie's past self filled it out. A Saturday at the end of the month does say "pick up granmum" and since Jamie's mother is not present, Jamie surmises she's somewhere before that date. *Kimmy would have said something. She likes mom.*

"Are you making those breakfast sandwich things?" Kimberly asks, almost erasing her mind from Bob's kibble path.

"But what year is...," Jamie trails off into silence. She drinks in the moment and lets her motherly instincts take over.

"You want one?"

"Yeah!"

"Okay, yeah...yeah...me too."

An adequate chef can grill Spam to resemble a decent hot-dog, but a seasoned connoisseur can transform the canned foodstuff into a delicacy. Right before the crackling fat renders, the addition of butter and brown sugar can candy the grease into a succulent puck of crispy fried meat. Sliding that onto a microwave warm biscuit and topping it with a folded egg is a heavenly morning concoction. A sunny side-up egg is Jamie's preferred method but a five-year-old isn't mature enough to appreciate a runny yolk.

"So, wait, Santa Claus is a no go, but you believe in the Easter bunny?" Jamie asks while sliding a plate to her seated daughter. Sketching directly onto her composition book, she pushes her drawing pad away to make room for her plate.

"Yeah. Santa's not real," Kimberly remarks with little hesitation.

"But the Easter Bunny?" Jamie rebuttals while flinging a washcloth over her shoulder. She finishes assembling her own sandwich, crushing it down to break the liquid yolk.

"He's a thing."

"Yeah, why the Easter Bunny and not Santa?"

"There are bunnies out there," Kimberly adds through her full mouth.

"There are also fat guys."

"But not magic fat guys!"

"What about magic bunnies?"

"Have you seen a bunny? They're fast and smart. Easter Bunnies don't need magic."

"Oh, you think there's more than one?"

"Yeah."

"Oooooh, that does make more sense than a magic fat guy," Jamie answers on the pragmatics of folklore characters.

"Unless they're lots of fat guys."

"Well, there are but—" Jamie looks at the time and a thought interrupts her sentence. It's 7:18.

"Today a weekday?"

"Wed-nes-day," Kimberly chimes. "There's a 'D.'"

"Do you have school today?"

Kimberly nods as she chews.

"Are you packed?" *That makes sense. She likes mom more than school.*

Kimberly shakes her head "no" as she's barely halfway through her meal.

"Ah okay, you finish that, and I'll get your shoes. Hopefully you can get them on before the bus."

"Can we bring Bob?"

"Of course we can bring Bob!"

The school bus rolls to a gentle stop as Jamie, Kimberly, and Bob jog toward it. "Alright, off you go," Jamie says, sliding Kimberly's hands through her backpack.

"Bye mum," Kimberly coos as if it were any other day. Kimberly tries to separate from her mother as the bus doors open.

"Hey, hey, hey," Jamie grips her wrist and tugs Kimberly back before she enters the bus.

"...I'll be here when you get back, okay?"

"Okay. Love you."

"Love you, too."

"Bye Bob."

Kimberly enters the bus and, even though she loses her daughter, Jamie waves as it drives off. "Kindergarten. So, five," Jamie's lips articulate but do not audibly pronounce. When the bus turns away, Jamie walks over to a nearby bench. She lets her ears take in the sounds of a quiet neighborhood. "Oh wow...oh wow...this is um...wow," is said while she gets comfortable on the bench. Bob does his best to hop on the bench, but his stubby anatomy forbids it. "Oop, hold on."

Jamie gives Bob a hoist and he nestles himself next to her. Both nostrils. Jamie can breathe through both nostrils. She forgot she used to be able to do that and the sensation is euphoric. *Is this the way you're supposed to breathe?*

After a moment and a few voluntary deep breaths, Jamie's eyes glaze over in elation.

She scratches Bob's chin as she uses her forearm to wipe away tears. Jamie can't help but smile at the sight of moisture on her sleeve. She presses the damp cuff against her lips and the joy overwhelms her.

"Oh, wow. Heh." *This is late spring, so this is the summer coming up. I'm picking up mom for graduation. That's what's going on. We go on our first haul this summer. Kimmy'll come, it'll be great and I'll make sure it doesn't happen. It won't happen. Never. Never ever again. Then everything will be different. I don't care how or why this is happening, I'm not going to screw this up again. Everything will be different.* Tears well up to their breaking point and Jamie rubs them away once more. Lowering her wrist, she meets a metallic grey ceiling.

Stunned by the sight, she finds that she's on her back. The breeze is gone. Bob is gone. The air is stagnant and stale. With eyes still moist, she surveys her sudden surroundings. The bunk of her 18-wheeler.

In a pair of shorts and a long-sleeve shirt, Jamie sits up in a panic. The bed in her cubby is missing its comforter and her thermos rolls off her chest. It lands on the floor, and she's not prepared for the volume of the thud. Her nostril sputters mucus while the other remains sealed. Her eyes are sunken with a dull sinus pain pressing against the inside of her face. A guttural groan escapes through her clinched teeth. Jamie looks down at her sleeve. There's moisture from her tears. Involuntarily, her throat pushes out a shriek that resembles a siren.

"Fuck...fuck...please...," Beyond frustrated, Jamie vehemently claws her way out of bed. Bungee cords are stretched in between the bunk and the front seats. Jamie muscles through the obstacle.

"Ah! What!? What's up? We good?" Anita awakens in a groggy alarm.

" Shit! You're-I'm-Shit!" Jamie belts. She all but forgot about her guest. Her first waking image is of Jamie tackling the gauntlet of taut bungee cords. "No, yeah, we're fine. Back to sleep," Jamie declares, fidgeting with the door handle. Anita's seat is reclined, and she's encased in a blanket. "Sorry! Sorry!"

"What's up? You alright? Are you awake or is this what I'm supposed to watch out for?" Anita attempts to ask before Jamie exits and slams the door. "Wow, okay," Anita comments with sleepy eyes facing a closed door. Due to the seconds of inactivity, Anita rolls back over and cinches the blankets between her knees and her knuckles under her cheek. She almost falls back to sleep before Jamie opens the door, grabs her phone and slams the door again. "Oh, wha? Jesus."

Hyperventilating, Jamie marches back and forth to find a steady breathing cadence. Images of her current living situation brand themselves onto her brain. She will not get a second chance. She'll finish this job and return to her routine. The dishes will remain in the sink. The trash will only continue to pile. They're there now. Waiting for her to return. The grooves in the couch and bed are waiting for her useless body. The only places that'll accept her. The only two places she can fit. She feels it. Her posture shrinks back forward. Her lower back twinges. Her body is preparing her mind for gloom. Her natural state.

It's as certain as the rising sun. She'll sleep until 2 p.m., move to the couch and watch re-runs of reality television while eating multiple orders of take-out, take the only walk of the day to the liquor store, return to her bed to drink her bottle of cheap whiskey and sporadically fall in and out of consciousness until it's 2 p.m. Every attempt to break this routine has only amplified its intensity. She had a glimpse of an escape but now it feels unavoidable. *Do that until your body gives up.* Prolonged execution by cowardice. Burdened by the shame, she can't help but feel she deserves her sorrow. The flicker of hope was merely there to reinforce her punishment.

She forces long deep breaths as she dials her phone with trembling fingers. She fails a couple of times to dial the right number, but when she succeeds, the phone rockets to her ear. It rings.

A befuddled and hazy male voice answers, "Hello."

"Hey, George. It's Jamie."

"Jamie...what, do you know what time it is?" George disappointedly asks.

"I know, I'm sorry about that, but can—" Jamie tries to ask as she nestles the phone between her jaw and shoulder.

"Are you drunk?"

"No, I just wanted—"

"Have you slept or have you been up all night again—"

"Listen, stop. I'm fine. Can I talk to Kimmy?" Jamie pleads with the dubious George.

Jamie whacks her knuckles together as she waits for a response.

"She's asleep. We're asleep. What do you want, Jamie?"

"I just wanted to see how she was doing. It's been a while."

"She's fine. We're fine," George unenthusiastically answers.

"How are drum lessons going?"

"She not taking them anymore."

"What? Why not?" The force behind Jamie's strikes increases.

"What disposable income am I supposed to have after my Lawyer's bill. Which I guess we can thank you for."

"Come on, don't say 'we'," challenging the implied shame in George's semantics.

"Well, she's not taking lessons anymore."

"You can't do that. She fucking loved drums," Jamie continues.

"I know, which makes you more of a bitch for how you handled this."

"Let's split it."

"That offer passed, Jamie," George states followed by an audible sigh.

"But, I can—AH!" a stiff crack in her knuckles interrupts her own argument.

"It's alright, Jamie, really. I'll tell her you called," George's voice evaporates at the end of the sentence as he presumedly lowers the phone.

"Wait, George?" Jamie begs. Nothing. "George?" Not even the static of a distant room tone. Jamie hangs up and lets her eyes slump down to the ground. The pain in her right knuckle swells and the thought she may have broken something leaps onto her pile of pessimistic worries. She attempts to shake it away, but nerve pain lacerates its way from her hand to just above her elbow. She makes a fist and squeezes. With eyes closed, she directs all of her senses to the pain. Severe enough, pain can drown out the voices.

It's not an ideal or healthy strategy, but the self-inflicted agony works. Her eyes open to a still flustered but cooler temper. She looks over to the truck stop diner with a sign that reads "Midway Diner." They're open and serve breakfast twenty-four hours a day. A chalk sandwich board proclaims that they now have "breakfast burritos". A bold claim considering you would only need salsa and tortillas.

Jamie opens her fist, rolls the injured wrist and shuffles over to the diner.

The sizzle of the flattop is audible when Jamie opens the door. She can see the senior stewardess waddle over with a menu under her arm. When she enters, an entirely different smell and sound strikes her ears and working nostril. She turns and pauses in reluctant disbelief. The neon. The dull vulgarity-laden chatter. Even the uneven wood underneath her feet. Jamie, not five minutes awake, is inside a bustling Pic-A-Lilli's Inn. Lou is tending the bar and it appears to be night from the lack of light penetrating the windows.

"Well....," Jamie combines nodding and shaking her head in one repeated motion. "...fuck."

She pushes against the wooden door, walks through and closes a metal and glass door. Sunlight is now on her back. Jamie has returned to the truck stop diner. She looks up at the sign that reads "Midway Diner" and then opens the door a crack. Sizzling hash browns and a confused waitress awaiting her entry.

"Well, fuck," she mutters as she walks back into the "Midway Diner." She looks at the clock inside of Pic-A-Lilli's and then her phone. They both read 10:35 p.m. Her hand hasn't left the doorknob. Nothing transforms, shifts, or mutates. It feels like a reality edit during a blink.

"Well...," She steps back outside, refusing to blink. "...
fuck." *When in the hell did that happen?* Jamie looks at her
phone. It reads 8:12 a.m. in the morning sun. Throwing her
sanity and comprehension of physics to the wind, she confidently walks into "Midway Diner" and/or "Pic-A-Lilli's."

Jamie makes her way over to the bar and ignores the surrounding social activity. It's right before last call the truckers
leave and the bikers congregate. Once the bikers enter, they
won't leave until last call. Leather and denim is not in short
supply. She sits at the same stool where she dealt with Lou.
Speaking of Lou...

"Hey, Lou," Jamie greets with a ginger dash of camaraderie.

Lou's expression is blank, as if he's never seen this person
"...hey."

"Jamie," she motions toward herself along with a shrug of
the shoulders.

"Okay...hey, Jamie."

"How goes it?"

Lou also shrugs as an answer and picks up the momentum
of the transaction. "What can I get you?"

"Coffee if you got it."

"Ugh," Lou looks toward the cash register where a Jimmy
Carter era pot keeps cheap coffee at a scalding temperature
"...I do, it's been on the pot for a while."

"That's okay. I'll have another shot of whatever, too, I
guess," Jamie says, knocking on the bar with her good hand.

"You have a brand?"

"Whatever you usually give me," Jamie requests as she
turns toward the bar. Lou ponders to himself as he studies
Jamie. The internal debate concludes and Lou nods in compli-
ance with his new customer. He walks off and pulls an empty
glass from the bar as he does so.

That door. That door is a Pic-A-Lilli's door. Lacquered
wood but lighter than you'd imagine. Jamie ruminates on the
door, convinced a sunny parking lot is on the other side.

Jamie exhales and turns back around to the sound of a
mug clinking on the bar. Lou places a cup of coffee in front
of her, a small bowl of creamers and two packets of sugar.

There's a fairly substantial chip in the corner of the mug that's permanently stained by coffee. If not careful, an unsupervised sip could draw blood from its finest edge.

She brings the coffee up to her lips. The impregnable nostril allows access to some steam. The pleasure of her first sip is intercepted by the sight of something to her right. Her head follows her eyes, and they gravitate to her booth. Something is in Carl's seat. She puts her coffee down to fully absorb what she sees.

It's by itself so it's apropos that it's playing a game of solitaire. It doesn't need two hands to shuffle its deck of cards. Age-tainted, the dull, off-white deck fluidly intertwines between the creature's sprout-riddled hand.

It seems to be made of a twisted cluster of tree branches and car parts. Its "skin" consists of mostly organic materials with branches and twigs braiding together to form arms, legs, and a misshapen head. Its perforated wooden exoskeleton reveals glimpses of its rusted organs. Gears and spare auto parts interlock and gyrate inside the creature, propelling its motion in a lurching fashion. For all of its locomotion, inside and out, the snaps and crackles of its anatomy are no louder than an air-conditioner on its lowest setting.

As it casually deals out its card game, it smokes a wooden pipe. "Smokes" is a loose term as smoke doesn't expel from its tobacco chamber or "mouth." With each inhale, the contents of the pipe glow a hot phosphorus blue and a gentle current of electricity fills the creature's innards. From there, the current disperses throughout its limbs and dissolves in its mechanization. The exhale is equally mesmerizing. A haze of phosphorescent steam leaks up from the figure's porous skull and dissipates in the air.

Jamie can't help but stare and wants nothing more than to see this automaton drink its glass of water. *Why would it drink water? Wouldn't it be gas? Or would the equivalent to water be oil? I guess gas would be food for people and oil would be water for whatever the hell that*—when its tungsten filament eyes glance over at Jamie, her fleshy ones shoot to the floor.

Jamie spills coffee in a half-assed attempt to act natural. Looking straight ahead with all her willpower, Jamie indirectly stares at Lou's torso.

"You good?" Lou asks.

"Hm, yeah, mmhm. Yeah. Yup. Thanks," Jamie snips.

"...Mm," Lou hums as he walks to another customer.

Jamie slowly sets her gaze back on Twigs. It's back to its game. There's barely an empty table. Why isn't anyone else gawking at the mechanical tree monster playing a card game? More disappointingly, however, it has a little less water. Jamie missed the mechanics of how it drinks. The lack of commotion over the creature along with the time and space-traveling phenomenon draws Jamie to a conclusion. *This isn't happening. This is me. This is my defective brain's fault.*

A shot of something brown slides next to Jamie's coffee. "Um, ah...," Jamie interjects, watching Lou put away a bottle of whiskey. "Ahhhhh...," the stress keeps Jamie's words from finding shape.

Lou gives Jamie a glance and looks over at Twigs. The sight of an anthropomorphic amalgamation of shrubbery and junkyard scraps doesn't seem to faze him. Flustered by the idea of not only being delusional but being robbed of a natural rapport with Lou, Jamie pushes herself away from the bar. She opens her wallet and scoffs at the absurdity of currency. The entire wallet flops onto the bar and Jamie makes her exit.

Jamie steps outside, into the daylight, and looks toward her truck. Devoid of motion, she assumes Anita is still sleeping. Pulverized by conflicting emotions and realities, Jamie falls onto a bench. She's doesn't sit, but her peripherals identify a bench. It's enough information to let her body topple into it. She bites down on her forearm and screams a high-pitched plea for sanity. Spitting and clawing lint from her teeth, she digs her free hand into her front pocket. She pulls out her phone and spins through her list of names. The phone stops at Sally's information. She puts the phone down screen up on the bench seat beside her. Contemplating hitting "send," her knuckles meet. Then again. And again. No longer internally deliberating about calling off the freight, she's become hypnotized by the numb rhythm of self-harm. The skin on her knuckles begins to peel, but her dread softens the pain. The growling of a dog is heard as Jamie's sanity descends into a coil of madness. Her knuckles crack again, but she persists.

I have never given up on a delivery. Through a pregnancy or a mental breakdown, I have always plowed forward. Sally will understand. She's a friend first. She was impressed when I came back with that shattered window? She even drove me to the hospital to get my hand stitched up. She cites that as an example to other drivers. Or was that supposed to be an example of what not to do? Maybe? She still goads me about insurance. No. It doesn't matter. If I didn't give up then and am giving up now, she'll know it's significant. She'll know the difference. She must, right? But how long do you keep a driver on that's a hazard to themselves and others? She won't hire me again. She'll hire others. Less reliable but less of a liability. Then what do I do? Never leave that apartment? I'll die. Maybe I should? But then I won't be able to afford Kimmy's lessons. I won't be able to afford them now if I don't finish. It's not great but I do have a life insurance policy. That'll pay for them. Maybe I should let this job kill me-

The sound of the door opening gives Jamie pause. She sighs with humility but cringes from the tenderness as she reaches for her phone. The stinging in her knuckles forbids the dexterity to slide the phone into her pocket.

Then a soft wheezing breath asks her a question. "Would you take objection if I joined you on this pine divan?"

"Nah, I was just about to get up anyhow," Jamie answers with the intent of standing. Looking up at the gentle voice, she finds her legs lack the momentum to function.

"Pardon my intrusion. I did not intend to interrupt or expedite a moment of privacy," the person made of car scraps and tree branches states. It politely stands by the edge of the armrest, allowing Jamie to reconsider.

"...No, you're good," *I don't think it can eat me.*

"Much appreciated."

Jamie looks up to see Twigs. It is taking the seat beside her. "Ah...um...," Jamie slips as the creature maneuvers like a hydraulic marionette. Ghostly in its motion, but precise in its execution. Jamie assumes its body would have to course-correct after constantly overshooting its movements. Not the case. Its mechanical innards are more intricate than they appear.

"Oh, this seat sits well with this old scrap." Twigs unlatches its pipe from the end of a branch on its shoulder. "The establishment's policies forbade me from smoking inside."

Twigs dabs a water droplet from the rim of its eye and drips it into the pipe. A blue light glows as it inhales. Jamie tracks the glow as it descends into its mechanized innards. "Technically this isn't smoke, but I thought it wasn't worth the argument." Twigs glances over to see an awestruck Jamie.

Realizing she's being rude, Jamie does her best to act like sentient garbage isn't peculiar.

"Ah, yeah, I used to smoke the E-cigarettes but it still felt weird indoors. Trying to be polite, I guess."

"Exactly my sentiment. Did they aid you in weaning off the fire?" Twigs asks with the warmth of a grandparent.

"Um, the E-Cigarette?"

"Yes."

"Yeah, I never really dabbled with regular cigarettes, but I tried to use it instead of snacking."

"Inventive."

"Since they had like brownie flavors and such, I thought it would work, but you know, one vice for another."

"But did they fare well against your proclivity?"

"Heh, take a look," Jamie motions to her less than sterling physique.

"Oh, balderdash, I find you quite vexing."

"Ah, it's not even about body image. It's profound how much I don't care about a thigh-gap. It's more about the health you don't see," Jamie reveals, discovering the values of an authentic conversation.

"Well, this would be damaging to you...," Twigs refers to the pipe but grabs another from its shoulder. Camouflaged in its winding body, Jamie didn't even see the second pipe. "... but I have a Portland briar leaf with a blend of skullcap, rose pedal, and owlbranch stem. It's quite ataractic and owlbranch doesn't even grow in this realm."

There was a time Jamie would try any narcotics offered, but one "not of this realm" may be dodgy. "...I'm okay. Thank you."

"The owlbranch is hypoallergenic to organic life if that should ameliorate your concern. In all certitudes, it more than likely will relieve mild symptoms," Twigs adds.

"That's very nice, but it's—I'm fine. Thank you."

"It's here if you should change your mind." Twigs places the briar pipe back on its latch and it smokes its actual electric cigarette.

Feeling impolite, Jamie continues the conversation. "So how are you by the way?

"Oh, fine I suppose. Just trying to pass the time as time tries to pass."

"Huh. 'Time tries to pass.'""Indeed."

"Neat," Jamie tries to hold her own with her wooden company.

"And you? How are you faring?"

"Oh, not great, I suppose," Jamie answers. Normally, she would forego the use of "I suppose,' but Twigs' vocabulary encourages Jamie to try more syllables.

"Is something ailing you?" Twigs refers to her hand as she intermittently shakes away the pain.

"Ugh, yeah, it's just...I've been routinely failing on top of myself these days...and years."

"Entropy is the law in this quiddity."

"Yeah, sure 'quiddity.' Why not,   I guess. It's just that my outlook gets hopeless, you know? No matter the angle."

"Boundless chaos never rests in challenging our better nature. A sentiment I, for one, can grok with," Twigs exclaims with a flourish in its bark.

"Yeah?" Jamie just assumes the word "grok" means "share."

"Mmm hmm."

"I had a feeling," Jamie deadpans.

Initially believing it was choking, a raspy and metallic groan expels from Twigs. It is comforting to Jamie that Twigs can laugh, and is laughing. Twigs takes a long toke from the pipe and nestles, in more ways than one, onto the bench. The pipe is not that alluring to Jamie, but Twigs' calm is certainly inviting.

"Does your offer still stand?" It's hard to register, but Twigs animates with excitement at the prospect of a smoking buddy.

"Without question. Just afford me a moment," Twigs comments as it unlatches the pipe from its shoulder and unlocks a small wooden compartment in its chest.

I think that was an ashtray from a car, Jamie thinks to herself. Inside is an herbal collection of weed that Twigs gathers and packs into Jamie's pipe. There's nothing in there that Jamie would consider "alien." She's more in awe of the herbs at an Asian supermarket than something not from this earth.

"I'll add a pinch of refined whisper tuber. It may ease the pangs in your digits," it mentions. Twigs keeps its eyes, which are fragments of broken lightbulbs, on Jamie's pipe. Its arms remain motionless as the sprigs of its wrists pack the pipe.

Jamie looks down at her battered hands. "Um, thank you."

"Here you are. Do you have fire?" Twigs hands the pipe to Jamie.

"I'm afraid I don't," Jamie answers, taking the pipe. It was smooth but somehow not lacquered. It's almost like driftwood but with a finer grain.

"That's quite acceptable. You'll have to provide your lungs though. I want to save you from the phosphorus burn."

"Um, okay-dokey."

Twigs inserts its fingertip into the nape of its neck and exhales. There's a small smolder of light outlining its visible bowls. "Here we are" Twigs retracts its hands, and its fingertips emanate a benign cinder. "And without objection; a graceful inhale when applicable."

Slightly worried about the consequences of smoking alien weed from a monster, Jamie finds the light near her cheek "That doesn't, uh, hurt you or—okay." Jamie's confusion is overwhelmed by Twigs' politeness. *If this kills me, at least it would make sense,* Jamie thinks as she brings the pipe to her lips.

The herbs glisten with embers as Jamie breathes in.

"Gentle embers always make me smile."

Jamie exhales a white smoke "Wow...that's...ah...okay. Wow."

"Soothing yet devoid of intoxication?" Twigs dampens out his fingertips by quickly dipping them into his eyes.

"Yes, that. That sentence. Thank you, again," Jamie states as she sits back in her seat.

"My pleasure."

"Oh, wow," Jamie declares with a sniff.

"There are no undesirable responses. Physical or psychological?"

"Oh no, no—yeah, yeah, mmm hmm, it's just—both nostrils," Jamie inhales deeply, unabated by snot. "It's been a while since I could do that."

"I am glad it's guilty of your relief."

In a pleasant silence, the two merely enjoy this moment in time. Jamie opens and closes her fists in quaint satisfaction.

"You're a man made out of tree branches and car parts, right?"

"Mmm hmm," Twigs responds with the agency of chamomile.

"Just making sure."

"Indubitably," Twig says with pristine diction.

I wonder if his bark tongue, if he has one, helps with pronouncing words. It's like he memorized a thesaurus but hasn't practiced much with socializing. Comes off snappy though. Trippingly? Isn't that a thing? Yeah, it is. He says stuff trippingly Jamie ponders with her truck in her eyeline.

"Is that your vehicle?"

"Hm?"

"The semi-trailer-truck. The majority of your vision has been directed toward it."

"Oh yeah. She's mine. Or I'm hers. Either way, fully paid off and she's been good to me."

"And how does your current expedition fare?"

"I actually think I'm going to call it off and go back home."

"In actuality?"

"Yeah, this job has been more damaging than anything."

"Damaging in what regard?"

"You know...mentally." Seeing the pipe weed depleted, Jamie hands the pipe back to Twigs.

"Certainly, an anguish best avoided." Twigs nods and takes the pipe from Jamie. Twigs' version of a thumb and an index finger brush against the web of skin by Jamie's thumb joint. Much like the pipe, it's textually fine.

"I'm just afraid to do anything and I think it's making me lose touch with reality."

"Hm, lapses of sanity tend to solve the occasional problem," Twigs mentions, cleaning the pipe of ash.

"That doesn't sound right."

"Well, what burden is failure when you've already failed?" Twig latches the pipe to its shoulder and leans forward. "It also sounds as if you have an opportunity to defect from that destitute regimen," Twigs advises as it stands.

Jamie just blankly stares back at him as an answer.

"I always have a spare pipe, a deck of cards, and words for conversation."

"Uh, thank you. Same here. Except for the card and pipe."

"It's been a pleasure." Twigs walks off and Jamie is left to herself. She looks over at the phone in her lap. Even though the pipe weed cooled her nerves, Jamie surmises it wasn't bequeathing her bravery. Instead, the weed hushed her apprehensions just enough for support to resonate. Jamie picks up her phone, dials and hits send in one action.

"Jamie, come on," George answers.

"George, just take a quick a second and listen."

"Jamie, if this is going to become a routine I'm—"

"Get her back into drum lessons."

"Ugh, Jamie, that's not really feasible," a defeated George grumbles.

"I'll pay for it. All of it. Just be a dad, get her there, I'll wire you money."

"Come on. What are you—"

"This isn't a discussion. Kimmy wants them, she gets them." Jamie interrupts.

A long breathy pause slithers through the phone followed by the ruffling of fabric. He is still in bed and Jamie has been interrupting his morning "...okay. I see the money, she'll go" George folds.

"Just get her there, George. It's all I want."

"Fine."

"And are you swabbing Bob's folds?"

"Uhhhh-that's kind of-"

"Don't be a fucking overdelicate prick and swab Bob," Jamie demands.

"I just don't know if—"

"If you don't swab Bob, the friction will scab and he'll get infections. Then you'll have a sick Bob. Don't get Bob sick."

"Alright, whatever. Jesus." George regrets not lying.

"Tell Kimmy I love her and I'll see her soon."

George takes pause before a sincere response. "...Of course, Jamie. Of course."

"Okay. Talk to you later," Jamie hangs up before George has a chance for a rebuttal. *Don't fumble this* Jamie thinks as she puts her phone back into her pocket. *Ride this feeling as long as you can.* She marches back into the "Midway Diner" and it is, in actuality, the Midway Diner. A rare ping of nostalgia for George plucks at her gut. This wasn't the diner, but their first meal was at something very similar to it. But just like every other memory, it unlocks doors to other more insidious ones in the corridors of Jamie's mind. *He wouldn't take his shoes off when he entered the apartment. He would floss in bed. He would always say "that's great" when I finished a story despite not listening. And eye contact. He wasn't much for it before, but I don't think he ever looked me in the eyes afterward. He only ever had that disappointed face for me after that. Glad I don't have to look at that anymore. Well, as much.*

At the sight of the sun beaming through the windows, booths made of torn leather, and a stained tile floor, Jamie feels nothing but relief. She marches her way to the counter and takes a seat on a stool. With a gentle grin and a knock on the table, things may be turning around for Jamie. *There you go. Proof. Healthy decisions, less batshit brain.*

Then she sees it in the corner of her eye. The chipped coffee mug and shot of whiskey she ordered. They're at the next seat over. She's roughly in the same spot she was in when this place manifested as Pic-A-Lilli's. She then looks over to where Twigs' booth would be for reassurance. The creature is not there, but his game of solitaire is.

"Here you go," a familiar voice responds.

Jamie turns to see the lackadaisical Lou placing her wallet on the counter.

"I took the liberty. In case you forgot."

"Um, thanks." Jamie slides her coffee over from the space beside her. When she looks down at her wallet and midnight order, she thinks *all that shit happened, I was just projecting a different place. We're all good.*

"You want some food?"

"Hmm?" Jamie asks with a prolonged hum. As Lou waits, he gently slides her whiskey back in front of her. "...breakfast burrito, please."

"Sour cream?"

"No thanks...Can I get fries instead of hash browns?" Jamie asks in a dreamlike state.

"I gotcha." Lou takes the receipt and puts it on the kitchen window. Whatever tolerance Jamie has stored is depleted by the sight of the chef.

"Dah! Holy Fuck!" Jamie exclaims as she rockets to her feet.

Through the kitchen window, a creature lurches its way to the ticket. This monster is seemingly made of arms, shaggy matted black fur, and a thick callous skull filled with teeth. Its skinless skull resembles that of a human's but its edges are more pronounced, jagged and tar black. The same cannot be said for its surplus of teeth. Less human and more akin to a shark's, the beast's jaws open at the sight of the breakfast order. More teeth. Rows of interlocking serrated bones spiral their way down its calcified gullet. In the place of flesh, where eyes should be, two anthropoid cilia inspect the paper. Once the crablike eyes read the order, one of its many arms tears the ticket away. The multi-appendage monstrosity reminds Jamie that it's very unlikely Lou would be here. *He doesn't commute three hours for a morning-shift at a diner, sleeps in his car and then does a nightshift at a bar.*

Everyone stops what they're doing and looks to Jamie. Stunned, Jamie just stares back. "...sorry. Arms. I um, banged my...elbow," Jamie stammers. Everyone goes back to their day. "My fault, my fault. Sorry," Jamie says as she lowers back into her stool.

It's hard to see its entirety through the kitchen window, but Jamie tries to distinguish if there are legs. As far as she can tell, the creature is a torso of slender arms with massive hands.

Arms places three plates of breakfast on the counter with three hands. At least two hands suspend it off the ground with a grip on something from the ceiling.

"Thanks," Lou answers to his coworker. He takes the plates off the kitchen window.

"Chat Chat," Arms chatters back to Lou. It clacks its predatory jaws together but doesn't seem have a voice. For such a terrifying visage, the chat language comes off as rather casual. Arms puts another plate of food on the counter.

"Ah, sorry," Lou apologizes.

"Chat."

Lou grabs the last plate and walks off as Arms fiddles away. It leaves Jamie's vision to presumably make her burrito. *The tree guy was nice enough. Maybe the Arm guy knows his way around a flat top.*

Jamie hears the bathroom door open and looks to see her wooden comrade exiting. Twigs gives Jamie a pleasant nod as it makes its way to its booth. Jamie nods back as she clears her thoughts. *What's he do in the bathroom? What's waste for trees? Carbon dioxide? What's a toilet do for that? Maybe the car portion needs an oil—*

Anita plops down next to Jamie. Her tired eyes look around the diner and she acts as if Twigs wasn't an anomaly "Phew, there you are. Thought you were...I don't know...something ominous."

"Oh I'm...," Jamie shakes her head as she reaches for the words. She takes the shot of whiskey. "...great."

"Right on. Drinking and driving," Anita comments as Lou motions to her.

"Something?"

"Coffee and I don't know...what'd you get?"

"Burrito," Jamie answers, putting her wallet away.

"A morning burrito?

"I have no fucking idea what time it is," Jamie remarks while folding her hands on the table. Her defeated timbre joins her sunken eyes to frown upon her scabbed knuckles.

"Breakfast burrito," Lou says. He registers the anguish in Jamie's demeanor.

"Ah, a Tex-Mex standard. Make it two."

"Deal." Forgoing the usual follow up question, Lou suspends the ticket on the kitchen window. Arms comes back to claim it.

Jamie almost jumps at the sight of the monster in the kitchen but tamps the anxiety down with her memory. Glaring over to Anita to gauge her reaction to the multiple appendage monster, Jamie's metric for sanity keeps ticking toward "unwell."

"…what?" Anita asks.

"Nothing." Jamie sips her coffee. Between the time traveling and the herbal intermission, the brew is still hot.

"Cool beans. Back in a sec." Anita spins around on her stool and springs off.

Jamie watches Anita scamper off. Once she exits Jamie's vision, Jamie rubs her eyes. Her fingers find her temples and she presses down, gritting her teeth. *That's not a tree-car man. You just smoked fucking hash from a bum and now you're getting anxious. Your stupid, already delusional brain is fucked out of its mind now. Good job. You're not going to finish this delivery because you're gonna wrap your fat ass around a tree because you thought it was a sizzler, you useless piece of—*

"…I see them too," Lou chimes, leaning his hands against the bar. Jamie looks up to Lou in awe. She refuses to say anything as this may be a trick of the mind. "Monsters walking around?"

"…?" Jamie refuses to believe the reassurance. The vindication would be too good to be true.

"There's a monster skeleton with seven arms making your burrito right now," Lou says in a mocking tone.

Jamie immediately retorts "And—"Jamie motions over to Twigs.

"A guy made of trees playing solitaire? Yeah, they're all over the place."

"And time? Has time been screwy for you, too?"

"I'm pretty sure I served Abraham Lincoln chicken wings yesterday."

"Where? Because—"

"That truck stop pub."

"Pic-A-Lilli's?"

"Yeah. Kept trying to leave, but couldn't."

"Wait, hold on. Do you know any fun facts?"

"What?" Lou asks, not expecting the question.

"Something's that's true. But, like, something I wouldn't know." Jamie has to lower her volume as it matches the intensity of her intrigue.

"Like what?"

"I don't know. Throw me some trivia, quick," Jamie stammers, concerned over Anita's return.

"Baseball fan?"

"Not at all."

"Know John Kruk?"

"Does he play baseball."

"He did. He has one testicle."

"Fuck yes."

"What?"

"I wouldn't know that, unless I'm imagining all this, and I made you up and that John Kurt—"

"Kruk." Lou corrects.

"Kruk has one testicle."

"...okay," Lou responds with a stone expression.

Surveying the area like a terrible spy, Jamie leans in "What, what, what, what what do we do?"

"Don't know. And not everyone seems to see or experience the same thing. But what I've overheard from the monsters is that they're waiting something out."

"Uh, yeah, that Twig guy said something similar. So, what do we do?"

"What were you doing before?"

"Making a delivery."

"Keep doing that."

"...okay. I guess. You're real, right? I'm sure you're not a figment of my imagination?"

"You're not, but I am."

"Am I?"

"You can't ask that if you weren't."

Jamie's mind wipes at the Cartesian doubt.

"Listen, most of them are pleasant," Lou continues.

"'Most of them?'" Jamie quotes with an underlying malice.

Lou nods to Twigs and Twigs returns the gesture. He motions to the pine automaton if it needs anything, and Twigs politely declines. "Some are fine. Some are pieces of shit. Some look like people. Like the one with you."

"Wait. Wha-What?" Jamie asks. Lou gets a glimpse of Anita coming back from the bathroom and walks off. "Lou? Hey. Wait, um, that's a really vague thing to walk off fr—"

Anita sits back down next to Jamie. "Hey hey hey."

Jamie turns to Anita as if she were the killer the whole time. "...hey."

6

"SO, ARE YOU GAMEY JAMIE?" ANITA ASKS, SEATED INSIDE THE truck. She struggles to find the hinge to upright the back of her seat.

"That's me," Jamie answers, closing her driver's side door.

"That's adorable. Like a Garbage Pail Kids sort of adorable." Anita puts on her newly purchased truckstop sunglasses. With both hands free, she attempts to operate the lever to her seat.

"Did someone try to CB me?" Jamie asks as she shifts into neutral.

"Ummmmm, Ironass?" Anita guesses as she readjusts her seat from its sleeping position.

"Hide? Ironhide?"

"Yes!" Anita chimes in, finding a tag on her fresh plastic sunglasses.

"Ironhide, yeah, he's a friend."

"Right on." Anita tears the tag off of her glasses.

"We'll probably meet up at some point today," Jamie mentions as she struggles to reach for something at the side of her seat.

"Nice, you guys do that thing where you draft or something?"

"Convoy?" Jamie gets a grip on her thermos.

"Yeah, that's the ticket."

"Not really. He wakes up at dawn and hits the road." Jamie swigs a mouthful from her thermos and sloshes the liquid from cheek to cheek.

"What?!?! That's outrageous! And not relish in the fine dining of...," Anita checks the name. "Midway Diner?" Anita says with exaggerated gusto.

Jamie swallows her makeshift mouthwash. "Eh, he eats one meal a day. The rest is nuts and fruit and shit while he drives."

"'Nuts'," Anita puns, "but that wasn't a bad place." Anita takes the plastic string from her glasses and threads it through her teeth.

"The diner?"

"Good burrito. Liked the vibe. Nice folks," Anita comments as she flosses with an unhygienic strip of plastic.

Jamie suspiciously glares at Anita as she stores her thermos away "...let's go." The truck pulls out of the parking lot.

Jostling movement invades Jamie's peripheral vision. *Oh Jesus, yeah* Jamie thinks. *Almost thought a bird got in.* Remembering Skull McCartney, Jamie realizes that he's looking directly back at her. There's little to question now as the accordion is a bit more extended than before. They head northbound, where the sun will meet an overcast sky. That distinct separation of sky looms heavy on the pavement. From clear crystal to miry clay. The haze hangs low but the rock crest mountains dwell listlessly on the horizon.

"Ah, here we go, here we go, here we go," Anita chirps at the advancing wall of rain. Then, a rush of metallic drumming floods the truck. "Whoa hoho, that trailer really makes this thing an echo chamber."

"Yeah. Almost need headphones if it's heavy," Jamie adds as she turns on the windshield wipers. In between each wipe, water overwhelms the windshield, blanketing the glass with a muted kaleidoscope of headlights and movement.

"Always liked that moment when you drive through an underpass on a rainy day. You get that quick pause of rain?"

"Well, we'll get plenty of opportunities," Jamie adds.

"Looking forward to—" Skull McCartney topples off the dash and lands by Anita's feet. "Whoop, I got it." Anita finds the prescription sleeve of pills on the pristinely clean floor.

They are wedged between the vinyl seating and the hard plastic of the center console. "Whoa, hello." Anita displays the sleeve to Jamie. "Found these, they look important."

Jamie looks over at Anita, holding up her pills. "Oh shit, just go ahead and throw them in the glove compartment."

"You looking for action on this gig?" Anita scandalously asks with a raised eyebrow.

"Fuck...put those away, please."

Anita opens the glove compartment to find several prescription packets. Around a dozen have been depleted while a dwindling pile remain full. Examining the pills, the glib innuendos whittle away with concern.

"Hey, get out of there," Jamie snaps.

Anita reads the long past expiration dates and looks to the cold Jamie. "You're not taking these, right?"

"Eh," Jamie responds with her apathetic eyes on the road.

"Wait? Are you?"

Jamie shrugs as her answer.

"Buy condoms. They do shit for our pleasure now, like get cold when cum hits them for some reason." Anita attempts to jest but the dower atmosphere denies the space of levity.

"They're not for sex."

"I think that's the only reason for them."

"It helps to...you know...manage stuff."

Anita shakes her head and blinks as if she were punched in the nose. "Periods?"

"I can't afford to pull over when I'm—you know...I don't want to get into it."

"Yeah, they suck, but you didn't take any on this trip did you?"

Jamie shrugs, nods, and then shrugs once more "Eh, I mean, no, not this trip."

"It is impressive how lazy that lie was."

"You won't get it."

"Still, come on, this can't be healthy."

"Taking a year off screwed up my work schedule and the erratic cycles and cramps weren't helping me get back on track. The pills helped me reset."

"Yeah, but that year was for a kid, right? Can't—"

"Please don't bring her up."

"Yeah, but that's why. It wasn't like you slacked off."

"Anita, please. I'm not talking about this."

"But, I know, I'm one to talk, but Jesus Christ, your liver. At least give your heart some room to catch a break. You could get clots and—"

"It's a part of the gig. You got deadlines. You meet them."

"Being alive gives you the perfect opportunity to make all of your deadlines."

A long, labored sigh rolls out of Jamie's mouth. "...I don't care."

"Jeeze, sounds like you never did." Anita's tone takes a dramatic shift on the border of hostility.

"Hey, what was that?" Jamie interjects on the border of insulted.

"What was what?"

"You know what. Don't be coy."

"Your attitude. It's getting exhausting."

"What's my attitude?"

"A bit nebbish."

"Nebbish?" Jamie reiterates.

"Yeah, like morose, but I like nebbish. I feel like nebbish works for you."

"Yeah?" Jamie's bitterness swells.

"Yeah." And Anita's matches hers.

"Because it sounds fatter?"

"Was that too coy?" Anita puts a period on her question by folding her arms, putting her feet on the glove compartment and staring out the passenger's side window.

"Don't put your feet up there," Jamie instinctively remarks.

With a wry glance and a click of her tongue, Anita drops her feet to the floor. The action's performed with a dramatic sulk. Similar to how a scolded toddler would perform for a parent.

The pulsating rain bombardes Jamie's nerves. With deep focus taken up by driving in inclement weather, only juvenile and shallow thoughts are accessible. "Did I insult you in some way?" Jamie asks.

Anita leans her forehead against the window. An infantile rebellion for having her feet on the floor.

"And where am I taking you, Anita?"

"North." Anita's breath fogs the passenger's side glass.

"And what's up North?"

"Just...let's just be silent for a little while, okay?"

After a moment of Anita's proposed silence, Jamie reaches to the side of her seat and retrieves her thermos. Leaving her eyes off the road for a precarious amount, Jamie finishes the contents of her thermos. Tightening the lid, she chucks the canteen in the back cabbie. It clangs as it hits the back wall and rolls under the bed. Jamie then rolls her neck and rotates her shoulders. Her left joint cracks with objection, but Jamie forces the motion with a vicious snap. They continue north.

<hr>

In the yolk of the storm, a patch of sun keeps the rain at bay. Jamie's truck is parked at a roadside rest stop. In an abnormal display of foliage, the southbound trees maintain a dark green pigment while their northbound brethren masquerade in the colors of autumn. Jamie sits where the orange, brown and yellow meets the green.

Indifferent to the ecologic anomaly, Jamie rests on a bench while tilting a bag of BBQ chips in her gullet. It's desolate. Her truck is the only vehicle in the lot. Cars and trucks pass by and they're accompanied by a buzzing splash of water on the wet highway. A gentle breeze rolls though. Jamie takes in the smell of wet pavement on a warm day. Emblematic but somewhat pleasant when compared to the stench of Sally's loading bay. Jamie looks up at the clouds.

A patch of gloom parts to reveal a shimmering blue underneath. "Oh, boy," Jamie unenthusiastically proclaims to herself. There are visible stars in the blue daylight. And on the edge of the silver lining, wisps of a celestial body of twisted colors. Either the moon is closer, or earth's orbit has a visitor. Jamie only catches a glimpse of the phenomenon before the clouds recapture the sky.

Anita silently walks up to Jamie from the rest stop bath-room. "Hey," Anita timidly rings. She sits across from Jamie. Her eyes are sullen and irritated.

"Hey," Jamie responds with full eye contact.

Translating the confidence for contempt, Anita's eyes find the wood of the bench "...Sorry."

"..." Jamie holds fast.

"Sorry, for my behavior, I guess. In the truck. That was rude. I just went to a bad place."

Jamie swats at the proverbial olive branch. "Who are you, Anita?"

"What do you mean?"

"Like, where are you from?"

"Where am I from?" Anita motions to herself.

"Yeah."

"Why?"

"Curious. You know I have a daughter and an unhealthy relationship with prescription sleeves. I know you once-in-a-while contact juggle."

"Ohio."

"Where in Ohio?

"Cleveland."

"Cleveland, Ohio?"

"Yeah."

"Does it rock?" Jamie says, mocking. "And what's your last name?"

Anita scoffs and recoils while sputtering "Sss-Silverstein."

Jamie's eyes perk up at the verbal fumble. "Oh, okay. 'Im-pressively lazy lie' or whatever you said."

"Jamie, come on." Anita punches her knuckles together.

"What the fuck was that?" Jamie hollers at the familiar sight. Anita takes a meek step forward and Jamie springs out of her seat.

"Whoa—fastest I've see you move—" Anita attempts to lighten the mood.

"No, seriously. Why'd you do that?" Jamie creates distance from Anita as if Anita were a physical threat.

"Do what?" Anita sincerely asks.

"You fucking know!" Jamie barks.

"Jamie, come on, I really really don't understand what you're getting at?" Anita pleads with an open hand tenderly reaching out for Jamie.

"You come on." Jamie's lost in the fog of resentment. "What are you? Are you even a person?"

Anita freezes at the question. Her once apologetic vulnerability armors itself in venom. Chaffing to the ground, Anita carves a chauvinistic smirk across her face "...you know what, Gamey Jamie? Do yourself and everyone you know a favor. Find a buffet and a jug of moonshine to murder yourself with." Anita gets off of her bench and storms off toward another one.

"Where you going?" Jamie yelps at Anita's back.

"North, you fucking idiot. North."

Anita doesn't even turn around and leaves Jamie with her bag of chips.

Watching her exit, Jamie crumbles the bottom of her bag of chips. She then pours the crushed remnants into her mouth, stands up and flicks the bag into the trashcan. *No way. Not a chance she's even real.*

Skull McCartney's accordion has expanded and his plastic eyeless skull looks above. Jamie stares at it as his head sways from the closing driver's side door. She bops his head to continue its bobble. Resentment festers as the head wobbles. After a moment of stillness, Jamie grabs Skull McCartney and throws him out of the driver's side window. She closes the window and turns back to find Skull McCartney back where he was on her dashboard. "Fine," Jamie says as she starts the truck. "Have it your way." Jamie shifts into first gear and rolls out of the rest stop.

Jamie solemnly drives alone. The truck approaches Anita, trudging by the side of the road. She continually attempts to get some momentum on her contact glass ball, but her rattled mind prevents her from getting it to contact.

Maybe I should—Jamie thinks before the memory of "do yourself a favor...murder yourself," echos in her head. *Nope.*

Good luck, Anita. Almost nice knowing you. Anita drops her glass ball and finds Jamie's truck passing her by. She gives Jamie the middle finger.

"Ugh," Jamie grabs her CB receiver. "Gamey Jamie to Ironhide."

"Go for Ironhide, Gamey Jamie," Carl crackles back.

Jamie clears her throat with the intent of inquiring about dinner, but Jamie chimes in through the CB speaker. Her own voice cuts through the static.

"Ironhide, this is Gamey Jamie, what's your 20?" The disembodied Jamie asks while the physical Jamie listens in disbelief.

"Gamey! Nice to have you back. I'm rollin' in on Pic-A-Lilli's," Carl responds to the possible specter.

"Wait...," the Jamie currently driving recollects.

"Be there in thirty," the voice of Jamie responds to Carl.

"'Be there in thirty.' Yeah. Alright," Jamie's déjà vu comes full circle. A parsimonious smirk creases at the ends of her lips.

"Yeehaw , 10-4 good buddy," past Carl continues.

"10-4," past Jamie replies.

The possibly tried-and-true Jamie grabs the CB radio and decides to respond to herself.

"Jamie?" Jamie squints, diving into the absurdity. "Gamey Jamie?" Jamie listens to herself decide to pick up the receiver. She pantomimes the actions she did while invisibly cheering for her past self to do the same.

"Go for Jamie," the radio crackles.

Somewhere on the edge of tears and laughter Jamie hollers "Yes! Fuck yeah!" Pushing down the receiver "I—Heh," Jamie has to collect herself before she responds.

"...go for Jamie," the radio timorously blips.

Jamie chuckles at her circumstances. Inhaling after the laughter, sorrow roars. Repelling her insecurities, she spitefully forces out a hellish guffaw. "...Hahahahah!" In a lapse of sanity or kindness, she howls into the receiver.

"Hello? What's your handle?"

"Hahahah...ohhhhh...she's not from Ohio, Jamie." Jamie's voice cracks and she holds back crying by biting onto her sleeve "She's not even a person," Jamie declares, throwing her receiver in the cab. "Argghhhh!!! Fuck you! FUCK! YOU!"

"Hello. Get back to me."

Jamie's rage batters the ceiling with her bruised knuckles as she wails in misery and universal loathing.

"...hello? asks her past self.

In her fit of anger, Jamie tears the CB receiver from the dashboard. Her wailing eventually dies down to a whimper. She closes her eyes tight in order to endure the anguish. Breathing deeply, she clings onto some kind of rhythm. She finds that her airway is blocked by a thick wall of mucus. She hocks it back into her throat, swallows it and continues to breathe. There. She finds it. Breath. She opens her eyes.

With the sun setting to her right, she turns on her headlights. Nodding a tear-kissed face, Jamie continues to drive north as the sky darkens.

7

I FEEL YA, BUD, JAMIE THINKS, STARING AT A FAST-FOOD EMPLOYEE.
Distraught beyond comprehension, he's mopped the same four
square feet of tile since Jamie sat down. His breath quivers and
his grip on the mop tightens. The most unfortunate bit is that
his compulsive mopping has unearthed how clean the floor
can be. The arid green fluorescent lights reflect an eggshell
white nowhere else on the floor. It's an overt contrast to the
musty plastic booths and water-stained asbestos ceiling tile.

Jamie, sitting alone, eats from a tray of crumbled wrappers. In her graveyard of fast-food remains, more than three
sandwiches have perished and the "fixin's bar" policy was
unashamedly ransacked. Now at room temperature, and the
mealy texture of upholstery foam, the oil-glossed paper bag of
fries acts as dessert.

A small whimper emanates where silence used to reside.
Jamie looks at the booth behind her. With salt-coarse white
hair and a tattered blue uniform, a sea captain quietly sobs in
a foreign booth. His hands are thick from finger to wrist and
his skin is closer to leather. His pipe and hat are placed on the
bench. Jamie is surprised to see the pipe isn't made of wood,
or the more stereotypical corncob, but clay. The fisherman's
cap makes more sense as it is shopworn in homespun leather.
This is a man carved by choppy ocean weather. Sun-bleached
and rough, his face only allowed a thin scraggly line of hair
to outline his jaw. His eyes are shielded from the elements

by wrinkles of bronze skin, an exaggerated brow and craggy patches of wild white eyebrows.

It is startling to see something so rugged weep in such a pathetic environment. Jamie outreaches her bag of equally pathetic fries. Two bright blue eyes look up at her from his sad slits. Jamie nods at the trepidatious sea captain. Inspecting the cluster of processed starch in his hand, the sea captain looks to Jamie. She nods and gives him a puzzling thumbs up. The sea captain returns the nod before he eats the fries. Baffled by the density of calories, he assumes it's some form of ration. They could certainly stave off starvation between distant ports.

Jamie looks into the paper bag. Only a few crispy french fry ends remain. She crumples the bag and points to the sea captain. Startled by the ease of folding paper, the sea captain looks to his beacon of the alien seas. She mimes eating more and the sea captain remains dumfounded and sullen. Jamie gets out of her seat while waving to the sea captain to join her. Uneasy and hesitant to make a decision, the sea captain remains seated. He cautiously surveys his surroundings and then to an open hand.

He attempts to read her hands. Silky yet not devoid of muscle. Manual labor with smooth glass, the sea captain surmises. Turning the wheel to a freight vehicle gave Jamie a sturdy grip, but combustion engines are beyond his scope. Accepting physical help from a woman would garner humiliation on the docks, but these are indeed strange docks on an even stranger land. More of a figurative gesture, he clasps onto Jamie's fingers as if she were about to curtsy. He never felt hands so soft, and Jamie never knew hands could be so rugged. How was it possible that his fingers could bend? His coriaceous skin could stop a tack. She wants to squeeze his fingers as hard as possible to test their durability.

He latches himself onto Jamie's arm as he stands. The walk as if she were walking him home from the bad side of town. The humming of the fluorescent lights causes him fright, but Jamie continues to shuffle to the counter. In awe of the teleporting Sea Captain and Jamie ordering him a bacon double cheeseburger, fries, bottled water for hydration and a choco-late shake, the fast food employee drops his mop.

Jamie drags a large soda and a paper bag into her bunk. Kicking her shoes off, she snuggles in the memory foam of her bed. She wedges one pillow into the corner and a second underneath her knees. She's on the hunt. The last prize before she can sit back into her hedonistic sanctuary. The baby blue pops from under her mattress. She reaches down and retrieves her empty thermos.

Unscrewing it, she sets it down on the floor and opens the paper bag. She then draws a plastic bottle of whiskey from her brown bag. With a twist on the cap and a snap of the plastic, Jamie takes a sip and refills her booze-rank thermos. The lip of the thermos is small enough to suspend the bottle of whiskey, freeing her hands. As the booze cascades, she pries out the re-maining seven birth control pills from her prescription sheet. She's made decisions this poor before and rebounded. Des-perate self-destruction has gotten her through arduous times a healthy body would have deemed intolerable. Therefore, her self-loathing is a survival mechanism and not a subconscious plea for love. Care takes consistency, time and reflection but hatred gets the job done. When the bottle empties, she shovels all seven pills in her mouth and swigs from her thermos of whiskey. Jamie knows how to navigate her suffering. She'll just endure her routine and do the least amount of damage to the people around her. At least her lifestyle will diminish her time as a burden.

She cringes as she positions the pills in her mouth to best be swallowed. With eyes closed and a congested inhale of the nose, she knocks the pills back. Five or seven go down easy as the remaining two get ensnared by a hoarse tongue. Hacking and heaving, she forces the literal bitter pills down.

"Ack, ugh," Jamie blurts, finding her soda straw for a chas-er. "Jeeezus," Jamie shudders, taking another shot from her thermos. With her ceremony of self-destruction on the down-turn, Jamie bundles into her corner.

Once settled, Jamie retrieves Kimberly's photo from her sleeve. She lays on her side with a pillow between her knees and props up the photo in her line of sight.

Her insomnia starts its nightly process. Exhausted, the first stage attempts to reintroduce the prospects of sleep. It'll be easy. It'll be comforting. It'll heal. But it always collides into mania. A vicious maelstrom of doubt and denigration repels the brain's benevolent intent. The once-heavy eyelids become spring-loaded with contempt. *The audacity of my own brain,* her subconscious shrieks. It neither wants nor believes it deserves such nurturing. Spiteful in its petulance, the mind replays every shameful act in a slideshow of torment. Teeth grind and joints seize. On a good night, this, coupled with tossing and turning, will be maintained until morning. Her current predicament, submission to vices and a vicious sense of despair ensure a bad night.

While staring at Kimberly's photo, darkness creeps to the edge of Jamie's bunk. Unaware of her buoyant surroundings, Jamie finds Kimberly's image floating away. The photo has switched places. This is the version that has both Kimberly and Jamie. She reaches for it. Jamie's arms are not as long as she presumes and the photo continues to distance itself. Instinctually, Jamie tries to yelp toward the vanishing photo but a cruel vacuum yanks the air from her lungs. It is in this state where physics takes on a vindictive and domineering identity.

As the photo echoes away, the swelling darkness atrophies the rest of the bunk. Jamie then watches the void devour her photo. Horrified by the sight, Jamie attempts to swim away from the abyss, straining to reach a surface. Any surface. Looking toward her feet, she finds that she's amidst the darkness. Endless, in all directions with only her body as a compass. She fixes her gaze straight ahead, hoping if she doesn't sense anything, she'd too fade into oblivion. Unfortunately, within that oblivion, stars emerge.

Vertigo strikes her stomach like a mortar. Jamie claws at the air, reaching for any form of support. The rim of her left hand clangs onto something metallic. Her thermos. It weightlessly floats away from her. She grabs at it, but it drifts away, propelled by her thrashing.

With alcohol literally out of reach, Jamie clasps onto her jaw. She opens her mouth wide enough to affix her pinky, ring, and middle fingers under her tongue. Her nails dig into the curve where her maxilla meets the flesh of the throat. Her tongue spasms and her gag reflexes convulse in primordial terror. Then, in a burst of desperation, Jamie unhinges her jaw. The skin on the edge of her lips tears, like the edge of a book, and droplets of blood form into weightless spheres. Wasting no time, she crams her left hand down her own throat. Teeth shatter and her jaw snaps further back into her sternum. Continuing her pursuit, Jamie's bad shoulder becomes her worse shoulder. It dislocates from its joint. The sacrificial act allows Jamie a few more inches of reach.

She then pulls her glistening forearm from her own pulsating maw. Partially digested food, blood, bile, and shattered teeth spew from her mouth. They form a cloud of viscera and Jamie has to spiral her torso to maneuver her face out of the organic mist.

Laden in depression, Jamie begins to eat the modules of food floating in the cosmos. She forces her jaw back to its natural position, but it's merely ornamental. She has no power over the dangling body part. It'll just catch food that her tongue can't shuttle to the back of her throat. After a moment of gorging, she catches bits of the food being devoured from something other than herself.

She sees no physical body, but a row of white jagged teeth attached to piercing yellow eyes. The sharp phantom feasts upon her entrails. What the teeth eat vanishes from existence into the impossible beast's digestive track. The sight gives Jamie pause. A separate row of teeth glides by her head and joins in at eating away at her innards. Then another. Then another. Before long, the cloud is being consumed by a pack of abstract carnivores.

One of the more ambitious creatures snips past its intended bite and draws blood from Jamie's thigh. It's dull, but there is sensation. Like the pressure of touch after anesthesia. The blood draws their eyes, and their teeth follow. Any form of defense merely offers food to the disembodied predators. Unable to flee in the emptiness of the universe, Jamie is torn apart by fangs with yellow eyes. Jamie attempts to holler. Even if her jaw worked, her deflated lungs couldn't hold a scream. That cruelty of physics makes sure of it. Her body is strewn across space in a cloud of blood and entrails.

Numb to the pain, she closes her eyes and embraces her dismemberment. She will not grieve the lost mortality. Freedom from responsibility is the prize and no longer regretting regrets is the challenge. Hopefully, there is not another side. This is it. Once the last morsel enters the emptiness of their stomachs, she will finally cease. Have the cosmos take her sacrifice of empyreal gore.

"Mum." Kimberly's voice murmurs.

Jamie grabs a hold of one of the dogs' jaws. She grapples with the teeth as it lunges for her face. Her daughter's voice brings sensation. Its falsetto brings pain. Distinct and certain pain. Jamie clings onto consciousness as she endures the horror.

"Mum," Kimberly's voice squeaks.

Emboldened by the weak treble of her daughter's voice, Jamie squeezes tighter, finding the beast's invisible larynx. Jamie's nerves explode with sensitivity. Gravity settles back into her vessel and the minuscule vibrations of air roll over her skin. Agony rushes through her veins, burning from the inside and freezing on the outside. The teeth and eyes lose their form as the darkness bursts with color and light. The amorphous orbs take shape and reality, once again, becomes real.

"Mu—" Kimberly's squeal is cut short along with her windpipe. Her skin tone is a pale blue with her tongue sticking out from her mouth. Jamie's grip tightens around the throat of her six-year-old daughter.

Jamie's eyes are open, dead, and empty. Unaware, she strangles with an unrestrained grip. As Kimberly's eyes begin to roll away into her skull, Jamie's hands are pried away from the child's neck. Fluttering back into consciousness, Jamie is hurled off of her bed by the same furious hands. She knocks into the nightstand and a clay bowl follows her.

"Jamie! Jamie! Jamie!" George barks.

George's salt-and-pepper widow's peak is the first thing Jamie can identify. His patchy scalp is what grounds her back to reality. George, shaken with panic, throttles Kimberly. " Kimmy, please baby, please. Breathe!" George tilts her head back into Jamie's pillow. Trained only by movies and television, George prepares to attempt CPR. "Come on, baby. Come on." Kimberly's breath returns to her. "There we go, breathe." Breathe. In and out." After a few gasps of desperate air, Kimberly lays still, digesting the motherly betrayal. Her face creases in sorrow and wailing fills the bedroom. George holds her tight and looks over to Jamie.

Awareness returns to Jamie when the shards of clay stop wobbling. "Oh no no no no no no no no, I'm sorry. I'm sorry. I'm sorry," Jamie stammers. She sits up and sees it again. The worst day of her life. She repeated the worst day of her life. Outside of her violent night terror, she looks up to her soon-to-be ex-husband. "It happened again. I still did it. It still happened." Color leaves her face, and her eyes surrender to misery. George's look of disgust is only second to Kimberly's look of absence. Those are not the eyes of a child looking at a disappointing mother, but a dangerous stranger. "God...," Jamie whispers as she slumps her head into her hands.

Smelling the bite of alcohol, Jamie lifts her head from her hands. She's no longer in her bedroom, but in the bunk of her truck. "...Damn it."

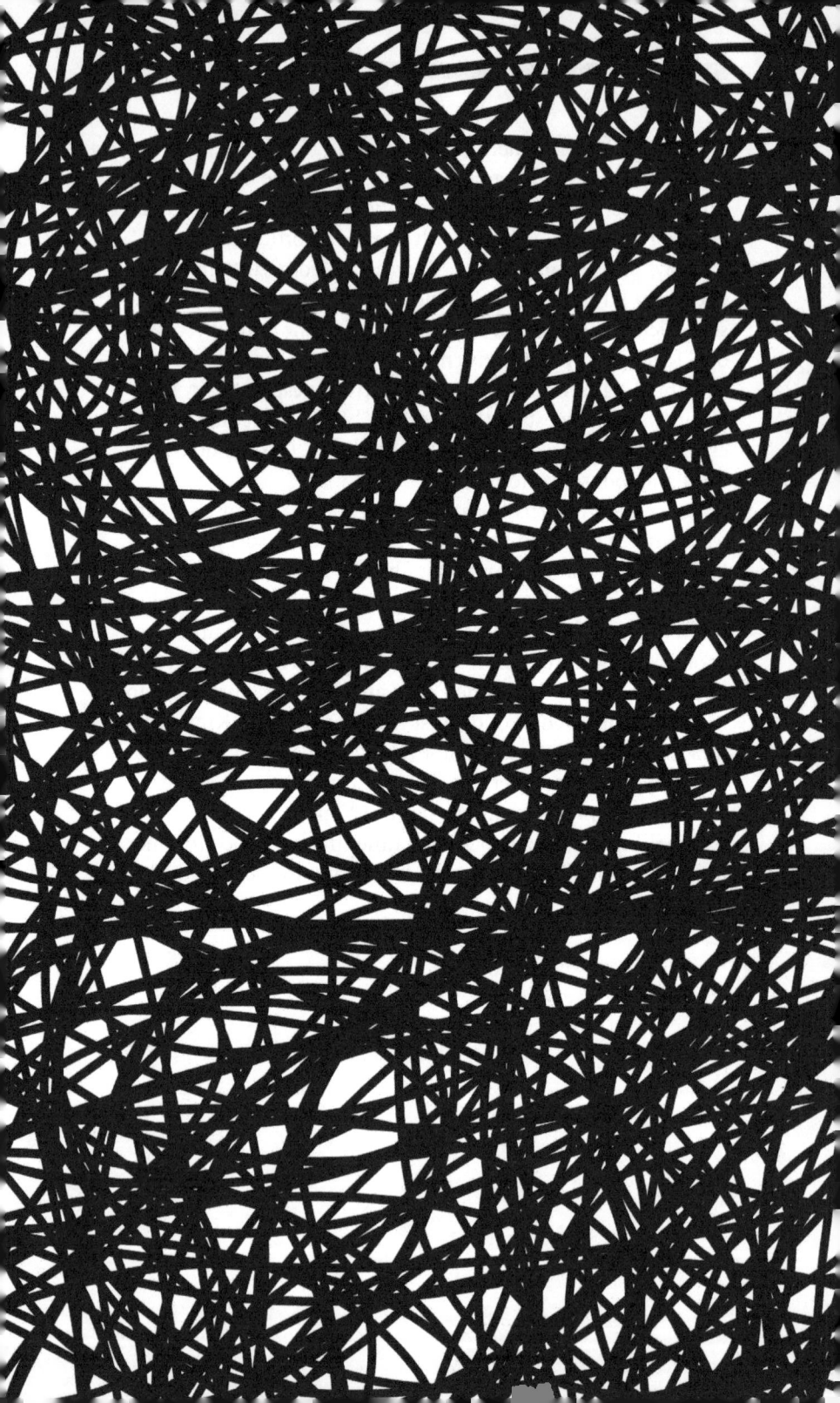

8

I DID NOT EXPECT THIS, JAMIE PONDERS TO HERSELF. SHE SITS up and grabs the picture of Kimberly. It's whole and how she remembers it. She gives her arms a quick glance to makes sure they're intact. Touching her face, she breathes in the smell of her own skin. Her left hand surveys her face to ensure the edges of her lips aren't torn. Whole and present, Jamie looks at the photo.

Not startled, not horrified, nor self-loathing, Jamie sits with a clear mind. Morose but calm and, more significantly, aware.

She slumps into the driver's seat. It's 1:14 a.m. and Skull McCartney's accordion is fully expanded. With a spirit broken-in by history, she bops McCartney's skull with a melancholic shrug. The glint of a smile quivers under sad eyes. "Hmm," Jamie coos as she starts the truck.

Jamie puts Kimberly's photo back in the visor and looks out the window.

The clouds have parted and the sky illuminates with celestial bodies of magnificent colors and twisted light. The earth seemingly has moons, and the southern horizon has what can only be explained as a galaxy rise. 400 billion stars and countless planets paint the horizon with a "glorious dawn."

Unimpressed, Jamie drives on, into chaos. Seasons flow and wildlife intermingles. Snow kisses cacti and owls perch on palms in the rural backroads of Connecticut. The silhouettes of mile-high sedimentary mountains reveal themselves from the east and the rise of an auburn-ringed planet from the west.

Jamie drives on, ignoring the shadowed giants lumbering above the trees. Thin and lumbering, they scour their foreign terrain with reflective eyes. They cautiously step toward open spaces to best maneuver around the wildlife.

The sparse beings of living light watch Jamie's truck pass. Shapeless and confused, the sentient energy mimics the headlights of Jamie's truck. Hoping to communicate their distress calls, they cower to a dim glow as she passes.

A scared dog with scales has joined a dwindling pack of Alaskan timber wolves. The impoverished band of predators investigate a sand-wash reservoir. Predators and prey alike discard their urges and regard this pool of freshwater as a sanctuary. In quiet solace, they congregate in reverence to support their shared struggle.

Jamie doesn't even turn her head. It doesn't interest her to see the cornucopia of beasts, earthly and unnatural, drink from the same basin. She's seen it. She's seen it hundreds of times. Seeing it act as a mirror to the swirling cosmos and nourishing life unseen by man is not worth turning her head. Jamie continues to drive onward.

It doesn't matter. Whatever is happening outside this truck, corporeal or imaginary, doesn't change what Jamie has and is doing. She is where she sits because of her actions, and she has a delivery to make. Straying from her path has ravaged her life so maybe fulfilling the task in front of her will right her course. Even with everything that has happened, at this very moment, she thinks *I wish there was actual coffee in my thermos.*

"Ah! Shit!" Jamie yelps. A wiry deer creature, on all fours, runs into the street. Jamie brakes and the truck screeches to a stop. The event happens soon enough to prevent the trailer from pivoting. The last thing Jamie wants to do is run down a helpless deer, monster, or wayward Billy. "Jeeeeezus!" Smoke from burnt rubber emanates from the tires and the truck stops dead in the middle of the street. "Fuck!" Jamie exclaims as her head whips back into her seat from the sudden halt. A fresh, yet not as severe, seatbelt bruise develops over the previous one.

When Jamie looks out of her front window, the deer creature remains in the road. Right outside of the headlights, the beast stands frozen in place. It's glowing reflective eyes stay on Jamie. Jamie honks, but it doesn't leave. It stands on its back legs and stays coiled at the mechanical monster that almost barreled it down.

"Oh shit. Look at you," Jamie says to the creature. Its horns are short and velvety. "Been a minute," Jamie rambles to herself, recognizing the creature from her walk to Pic-A-Lilli's.

She steps out of her truck and wrappers from truck stop snacks crumble onto the street. "Oh, jeez," Jamie remarks as she hurtles over the trash. "Hey! Shoo!" Jamie attempts to scare the animal as she stays beside the truck. The deer creature's ears point downward and its head lowers in caution. "Come on. Scram. It's okay." Jamie raises her voice, but her pitch is far too maudlin to be threatening. She steps toward it, and it lowers its front legs to the ground. "There you go. It's okay. Back to your monster family." She takes another step and scoots her hands in its direction. That does it. The creature scampers off before Jamie takes a step into the headlights. Her next strategy was going to be revealing herself as it may have been blinded by the light. Now outside, under celestial teeming skies, Jamie looks down the road. She sighs at the ethereal phenomenons. There's a glimmer of what could be a building in the distance. She holds her hand out. The vibrant night sky casts a shadow onto the ground and Jamie faintly smiles because of it. She holds her hand up to the sky. It's a pitch-hued silhouette upon the cosmic radiance. Still on her mission, it's hard not to take in the beauty of the bedlam. Fireflies mingle with floating bio-luminescent pappi seeds from dandelions are not found on any continent. They pass between her hand and face. Jamie watches them flutter by and that leads her into seeing an ambling crustaceous giant.

It slowly trudges its way through the forest. Its body is enveloped in shadow, but its skin seems to be reflective, mirroring the bombastic colors of the raging sky. Its appendages are taller than any tree, but it does its best to avoid breaking them. It walks on four spider-like legs and its head resembles that of a human's with long spindling hair. It's a horrifying visage, but its gentle stride quells its frightening appearance. The pincer points click against the asphalt and Jamie doesn't move as it approaches. The giant doesn't take notice of Jamie as it slowly passes the street. Jamie looks up at the towering creature as it continues its saunter. Its underbelly is soft and, right where you would assume a heart would be, beats as if it had one.

Jamie's gaze follows the monstrous entity into the woods and, in doing so, spots familiar creatures. About half a dozen standing deer are, and have been, staring at her.

"Oh, hey." They lower themselves to all fours and, as a herd, make their way toward the street. Jamie flinches, but crushes her fear with apathy. "Ugh, whatever," Jamie sighs.

Hunched over, looking as small as they can, the deer creatures cautiously reveal themselves from the forest. They enter the street and enter the light of Jamie's truck. Jamie can finally see the details. She only knew them as foreboding outlines with piercing eyes. Their features are frail. Their eyes sunken and their muscles atrophied. The exaggerated shape of their joints is intimidating, but seeing their flesh hang from emaciated bones washes away their menace.

Adjusting to the light, they gently step in the center of the street, presenting themselves to Jamie. There are five in total of varying sizes and shapes. For being otherworldly, their expressions are easy to translate. They are solemn and desperate.

Their faces, covered in fine fur, are narrow and more pronounced than a human's but less of a deer's. Reminding her of how the sea captain's face was etched by the ocean, Jamie imagines a world not unlike our own. A landscape where these animals wander in woods not unlike the Pinelands.

The alpha's thin grey fur comes to a point on his sharp chin. It looks as if a man grew the beard of a goat. He approaches Jamie with hesitation and fear in his stride. He struggles but rears to stand on his hind legs. it takes a moment for him to find his balance. Jamie instinctively reaches out for support, but only rears the family in fright. The alpha, coiled from Jamie's flinch, finds his bearings, and stands straight up. Jamie and the alpha make eye contact and he does his best to evoke their plight.

"...Um—" again, the alpha flinches at Jamie's attempt to speak. "Sorry—" and once more. "You don't have to—" The alpha, eyes wandering over Jamie's body language, eases to Jamie's ramblings. "It's okay, it's okay. Sorry." The sound of rustling interrupts their interaction.

Jamie keeps her shoulders square to the deer creature but cranes her neck over to her truck. A soft antlered buck and another younger creature have found Jamie's trash. On all fours, they lower their heads, inches off the ground, to inspect an empty chip bag and a plastic liquor bottle. The bottle forces the buck to reel its head back. The other's snout digs into the crinkling bag. She gently picks at her discarded junk food and shares what little crumbs are left inside. The elongated palms of their versatile legs can pinch from their thumbs to their index finger. Between their stout digits are curved retractable nails that resemble a hoof when they're walking but cat claws when they're standing.

The alpha looks over to his kin and then back to Jamie. "Okay....okay...I think I'm reading ya." Jamie nods to the alpha. She walks off and the five frightened animals dash back with what little strength they have. "Not hurting ya. Not gonna hurt ya." She steps into her driver's seat and grabs her keys. All eyes follow Jamie as she marches to the back of the truck.

Gripping the latch of the trailer's rollup door, Jamie hoists herself up to the grated platform. If there wasn't an unparalleled cosmic event bombarding her psyche, she would appreciate the ease in which she makes the step. The herd gathers around the back of Jamie's truck as she unfastens the robust enforcement lock. Swinging the hefty security gate aside, Jamie unlocks the door. "Alright, you guys are going to flinch again, but you'll be fine," Jamie remarks to the deer creatures. With a grip on the weather coarse handle, she rolls up the back of her trailer.

She was right. The deer humanoids scuttle back from the clanging racket of the retreating door. Construction equipment rests on one side and plastic shelves of packaged bread on the other. "Nice. Still here," Jamie comments as she steps into her trailer. The lone bulb, encased in a plastic sheath, guides Jamie with a dim tungsten glow. The illumination is faint and patchy as it's filtered through dozens of dead moths.

She holds a loaf of prepackaged bread into the light. As she does so, the deer creatures creep toward the back of the truck. *Fancy bread, indeed.* Multi-grain raisin is labeled with a telephone book worth of health benefits and organic history. She peels the plastic back to reveal another film of plastic. Pre-slicing not organic? Jamie quips to herself.

She twists a morsel of crust off the oblong loaf. She kneels down at the edge of the trailer and hands the piece of bread to the alpha.

"Hey, here you go." She sniffs it to reinforce its edibility. He's hesitant, so Jamie takes a small bite of the fancy bread and extends her hand. "You know, not my bag, but it's food."

The creature gently extends his hand and takes the bread. He may be on the verge of starvation, but his hands are still powerful. His knuckles are wrapped in an armor of fibrous muscles and the claws between them have pierced skulls and opened rib cages. *This is a dumb idea. This is dumb. This thing can fucking kill me. This is lame bread. I'm a fat fucking treat. Like if a turkey offered a cracker to a Kodiak bear. This makes that amount of sense,* Jamie thinks, looking at the beast up close. Jamie matches his fear as it takes the bread from her hand.

After inspecting it with fogged eyes and crusted nostrils, the alpha bites into the bread. His teeth bolster Jamie's anxieties. Much like a dog's, they're fanged in the front with molars in the back. He eats like a wolf as well. He shears a piece of the bread off and swallows it without chewing. The sight of dog teeth causes Jamie's spine to tingle and skin to shiver. *I can close the door and stay in here if they lunge at—* He offers his crust to the others.

"No, no." The altruistic act quells Jamie's fear. They all look to Jamie. "Have it all."

Jamie climbs back into the trailer and starts pulling out the shelves of bread. She tears open another loaf and offers it to the buck. They look to the alpha and the alpha looks to Jamie. "It's okay." The alpha waves them forward and they all start gathering the bread. "It's okay. Go ahead." Seeing a group of reluctant planet wayfarers graciously share their food, Jamie pulls the orange racks of bread from their compartments. She places them on the lip of the trailer.

"Hey, look at this." Jamie motions to the alpha. Dividing up the loaf, the alpha looks to Jamie. "Okay, there's plastic on these guys," Jamie mentions as she demonstrates how to open the seal of a loaf. He saunters to Jamie's side, entering a peripersonal space the two have yet to cross. He looks at the offering. There are dozens of loaves presented. "See." Jamie opens another. Watching closely, the alpha lifts one of the loafs and sniffs it. "You got this. Give it a rip." With the claws of his right hand, he peels back the membrane to find a crusty loaf of pumpernickel. "Ah, sourdough might be an acquired taste, but I think you get it."

Jamie peers around the corner of her truck and looks down the street. She gauges the distance of the building and looks to the feasting deer monsters. They now each have their own loaf and are kneeling in a circle as they dine.

Jamie steps inside her truck and grabs the picture of Kimberly and Skull McCartney. McCartney's suction cup drags across the dash before it submits to Jamie's pull. *Should I move to the side of the road?* When Jamie steps out of the truck, she gives the alpha one last glance. He glances back as he kneels down to his family's banquet. She then looks to the sky, exploding in activity. The forest is also teeming with life the earth has yet to dream of. *Eh, I'll leave a cone.*

Jamie reaches under her driver's seat and pulls out three orange traffic delineators. As she's about to close the driver's side door, her thermos sits in-between the seats. Moving the cones has rolled it into view and in that view, her logbook resides. The duo upend Jamie's compulsions as she hurls the logbook into the woods. She then looks to the thermos. The mere touch may set off a chain reaction of cravings. With an aggressive chuff from her nostrils, she leaves her thermos and closes the door.

Rolling her neck and shoulders, Jamie walks toward the establishment. She stays in the middle of the street to get the best distance possible from woodland predators. The cosmos dances above her as what looks like the transparent ghost of a nine-foot hawk watches from the trees. "Heh, of course." The establishment she is walking toward is none other than Pic-A-Lilli's. Even accompanied by gastly sights, Pic-A-Lilli is a monument to shab. Still in putrid green neon filtered through thousands of desiccated insect corpses and sparse in the way of vehicles, there's a plethora of movement through the windows. It's the movement of an at-capacity tavern. "Oh, boy."

Jamie enters a cornucopia of creatures, time travelers, and specters. Even though Pic-A-Lilli's is copious in activity, the volume remains manageable. The bonds made here are not that of familiarity but that of a common predicament. All are strangers that were torn from their homes and hurled onto a planet of strangers.

Twigs sits at a curved booth in the corner along with another tree creature, the seven-armed skeleton chef, Lou, and what appears to be a confused chimney sweep from 19th century England. Wearing all black, a wide brim hat and a face sucked in from malnourishment, the chimney sweep keeps his brush across his lap. He merely watches the card game while smoking from Twigs' pipe. Lou, Twigs, the other tree being and Arms are playing the card game thirty-one. They are using pennies from the tip jar as chips. It's an easy enough game to learn as well as to play.

Jamie stands by the door and looks down at her picture of Kimberly. Seeing the chaos, her buffer for the absurd reaches its threshold. Sustaining her level of resolve for the family of deer creatures has drained her confidence. Memory volleys her an image of her horrid night and the life that got her to it. Every decision she's made and didn't make has brought her to this moment. Unbridled chaos. She begins to cry.

Twigs' eye catches the familiar Jamie while the other stays on its cards. "Jamie!" Twigs chummily exclaims. Jamie raises her head and the glint from tears strikes Twigs. "Jamie?"

Jamie crumples to the floor and lands in a folded heap. Her head inches from the ground. Twigs and Lou come to her aid.

"Jamie, come to your feet. Come with us," Twigs proclaims. Twigs' branch supports her left arm as Lou supports her right. The velvety wood of Twigs caresses her arm so evenly, Jamie barely feels its pressure. Lou, on the other hand, has had years of hurling drunks out of diners, bars and musical venues. His grip could have been a vice clamp for all she knew.

"I can't...I can't take this anymore," Jamie moans to the floor.

Twigs and Lou help Jamie to her feet. "It's quite alright. 5th dimensional tesseracts tend to be savage to the soul."

"We got ya," Lou adds. Lou and Twigs escort Jamie to their booth. The patrons remain respectful and make room if in their trajectory. If anyone does make eye contact with the ailing Jamie, it's joined by a compassionate smile or the encouraging equivalent. Smiling isn't anatomically possible for some.

"Here we are," Twigs discloses as they shuttle her into Lou's seat.

"What can I get you?" Lou's bartending rote kicks in.

"I'm good, thanks." Jamie says as Twigs sits besides her.

"Jamie, this is a relative of mine. We don't really have names but he's pleasant nonetheless."

The other Twigs creature, Embers, greets Jamie with a nod. Its skin is comprised of more uniform pieces of birch bark and the primary gadgetry of its insides may not even be from a car. It may have been a riding mower or tracker by the size of the steering wheel embedded in its chest. "Greetings to you, Jamie," Embers says with a more cancerous and hoarse tone.

"Hello," Jamie responds.

"And this here is a man we just met, and he goes by the name of Fredrick." Twigs motions to the chimney sweep. Fredrick waves in confusion. "He's a bit stunned from being torn from his time period, but his spirits are intact."

"...Hi." Jamie says to the bewildered Fredrick.

"How'd you do?" Fredrick responds with the voice of a three pack a day smoker with pneumonia.

Jamie looks over at Arms. It salutes Jamie with four of its hands. Seeing it sit at a table dramatically decreases its malevolence. The lack of dexterity in its face but mobility in its hands reminds Jamie of a Muppet.

"Hey," Jamie extends her hand and it gently shakes back with three. "Good burrito."

"Chat chat," Arms chats.

"...yep." *Those were some amazingly moisturized hands.*

Lou puts down a glass of water and a shot of whiskey in front of Jamie. "Here you go," Lou says as he pulls up a chair to their booth.

"Uh, thank you." Jamie looks to the whiskey. Right now, it has the appeal of battery acid.

"So, how did you find yourself here?" Twigs asks.

"Um, I kind of gave up on the delivery thing. Well, I didn't really give up. There were deer monsters that I gave my shipment to. It just seems insignificant at this point," Jamie says as she sips her water.

"Then take the present to ease your senses." Twigs takes a drag from his pipe.

"Are you off the clock?" Jamie asks Lou.

He shrugs. "It got too nuts for me. I'm just going to fuck it until this is over." It's a paradoxical detail, but Lou's sleeves are unfurled and that somehow makes him look more casual.

"So, this is happening?"

"Told ya."

"And what is exactly happening? I'm not crazy?"

"No, no, no. Well, I can't speak for your mental state, but I was unaware that this was your first Reality Squall," Twigs explains.

"I'm not even going to pretend to know what that is."

"I've been calling it 'the Warp'," Lou adds.

"That doesn't help," Jamie chides.

"Wait until he tries to explain it."

Fredrick nods at Lou's comment as he hands Twigs' pipe back.

"Your universe has inflated into others. That over expansion breached into 5th dimensional space time so realties..." Twigs takes a moment to find the words. Embers takes the pipe from Twigs and begins to clean it. Its bark can intricately interlock without the use of branches. Embers turns the wheel on its chest and herbs sprout from its back. "...coexist as all of our universes right themselves. Imagine every universe eclipsing each other across dimensions."

"They physically, psychically and psychologically can't comprehend that," Embers interrupts.

"I'm not even going to try," Jamie adds.

"Apologies. But beings of the three-dimensional persuasion can comprehend the phenomenon in what some would consider a rather jarring experience."

"Hmm, 'jarring'," Lou repeats.

"...there's more than one universe?" Jamie asks.

"Yes" Twigs answers.

"How many more?"

"About an infinity."

"That's a lot."

"It happens every so often," Embers remarks, lighting the pipe with a heated copper coil ingrained in its palm.

"Some beings rather enjoy the experience. They meet new life forms and relive past experiences." Twigs assures.

"None of which is predictable or consented to, of course. He forgets to mention that," Embers adds.

"Yes, the phenomenon has the potential to be rather Mephistophelian."

"How long does this usually take?" Jamie asks.

"Time's kind of up for debate these days," Lou adds, taking Embers' offer of the pipe.

"We're at the mercy of reality," Twigs answers.

"That sounds horrible," Jamie comments mid-sip.

"Indubitably." Lou passes Jamie the pipe. She foregoes the drug and passes it Frederick. "What if this never stops for us?"

"It will one day," Twigs mentions.

"They may perish by then," Embers retorts. "Oh, yes. Apologies. Our essence is fifth-dimensional, so we occupy several planes at once. We constitute these vessels to abide by the event."

"It ain't so bad," Lou says.

"How the hell do you come to that?" Jamie asks.

"How's this that different from what we're used to?"

"Other than space and time unraveling and there's monsters all over the place?"

"Yeah."

"...we're helplessly caught in this space storm thing.""Reality Squall," Twigs corrects.

"Yeah, that. So, I think that changes and covers pretty much everything."

"Eh. Life was a chaotic mess of horseshit way before monsters started ordering curly fries." Lou takes the pipe from the offering Frederick.

"Ugh," Jamie groans.

"Nanty 'narking that pipe is, right, aye?" Frederick mentions in a dialect so thick, it could be misconstrued as a different language. Jamie assumes he's trying to say he likes the herbs in Twigs' pipe.

"'Soothing yet devoid of intoxication'," Jamie quotes Twigs. The two point to each other in a communal gesture.

"Aghhhh!!! AGHHHHHHHHHH!!!!!" emanates from the front door. Jamie looks over to see Carl. He has just entered Pic-A-Lilli's. On his knees, he hollers uncontrollably and grapples with his own head, succumbing to madness.

"Shit, Carl. Excuse me guys," Jamie says, fidgeting her way from the booth.

Before Jamie walks off, she looks to Twigs for guidance. "Uh, universes are smashing into each other and now times screwy and there are tree people?

Twigs shrugs and throws its hands up "Ehhhhh, it's more of a cosmic expansion, breaching fifth-dimensional space manifesting a tesseract for the 4th dime—you know what, it doesn't matter, that sounds adequate."

Jamie pats Twigs' shoulder as she walks off. "Copy that."

Eight minutes of explanation later, Jamie stands over the table with an awestruck Carl.

"Um, this is Carl. Carl, these two guys made of branches don't have names but they're nice, you know Lou, I've been calling this guy Arms because of all the arms and that's a *Mary Poppins* chimney sweep. What was your name again?"

"Fredrick," Fredrick answers, now enjoying a 21st century lager.

"Fredrick," Jamie reiterates.

"Uh...," Carl mutters. He's still mortified but he finds a word in the befuddlement. "Hello."

"Charmed," Twigs hails

"Greetings to you, Carl," Embers says.

"Chat," Arms chats.

"Carl." Lou says as he stands.

"Lou," Carl says as Lou offers him a seat.

"I'll grab you a water." Lou walks off.

"Yeah...that'll be...that'll be something," Carl utters as he sits down in Lou's previous chair. Jamie shimmies back into her seat at the booth right next to Carl.

Seeing Carl stunned, Jamie speaks. "Did you use your water weights yet?"

Carl eventually makes eye contact with Jamie. "Um, yeah, once."

"How were they?"

"Okay. But then I saw a guy with a big cat mouth for a stomach eat a fire hydrant."

"They'll do that," Lou adds as he places the water down in front of Carl. He sits in the chair next to Carl. Their booth is now at maximum occupancy.

"So, I ran back into my truck," Carl murmurs. Twigs hands him a pipe and Carl remains transfixed at the monster handing him tobacco. Carl and Arms make eye contact.

"Chat chat."

Blinking repeatedly, he looks behind him. There's what looks like a fox bat with a leather armor shell and a head that resembles an armadillo's suspended from the ceiling. It's talking to a woman from what can be described as a steampunk era future. His seat placement is a wise tactical decision.

Facing away from the expanse of the bar, and toward an immediate wall dressed with friendly faces, helps Carl transition to the new reality. Carl looks back over at Twigs. Unsure of how to proceed, he turns to Jamie.

"It's smooth and there's stuff that doesn't grow in this universe or reality or something. It won't fuck you up." Jamie explains. Carl takes it and inhales. The red tension in his eyes immediately sinks back to an eggshell white.

"Oh man. Oh man...don't know what that is, but...oh man." As Carl exhales, Anita walks through the door. Even surrounded by monsters, she walks with the composure and swagger of a trust fund billionaire.

Jamie shutters at Anita's entrance and she instinctively picks up her shot of whiskey. "Ah, shit."

"Beg pardon?" Twigs asks.

"Oh, that girl over there. I picked her up for a ride, but it ended up getting pretty fucking sour pretty fucking quickly." Jamie forces her whiskey back down to the table.

"Oh," Twigs says.

A more sedated Carl looks towards the doorway and then back to the group. "Oh, yeah, Kim?"

"What?" Jamie fails to hide the alarm in her voice.

"Yeah. I gave her a ride. That's how she's here. Kim." Carl reiterates.

Jamie's eyes widen and she blinks once for an extended period of time. She opens her eyes. "...What?"

9

DESPITE LOOKING LIKE HIM, THAT IS NOT MY DAD. YOU'RE GOING to have to do more than have a mustache to convince me. "When's that Cleveland internship start up, again?" he asks.

"Apprenticeship."

"Sorry, apprenticeship."

"I haven't heard back from the guy yet?" I answer.

"Thought you were going to help demo his studio?"

"I am."

"For that relaunch."

"Oh, I know."

"So, when was that supposed to happen?"

"Whenever I hear from him, George." That did it. That struck a nerve. But here's the deal, he just gives me a scowl and drinks his cream-less coffee. He didn't chuck it at me or call me a brat or bitch or what-have-you. That's not him. If the absent jowl isn't a tell, the lack of breaking another mug sure as hell is.

———

I tried to call the design studio again. This will be my sixth message. At this point, I'm just calling to confirm a rejection. That way, I could at least stop thinking about it. I'm still packed for the hell of it. I know I'm waiting for them to have a "meeting of the minds" before they make their decision, but why wouldn't that have happened by now? At this point, rejection would be cathartic. At least I'd know effort was taken and

I wasted somebody's time. Even if it's just a copy-and-pasted email with my name filled in. There's a victory there somewhere. While they are busy queuing up my "we regret to inform you" response, a separate design studio takes on the next Shepard Fairey. Too busy copying and pasting while his resume wilts in their inbox. Still, I packed though. I don't see the advantage of pretending to be hopeless. What benefit is there to be literally devoid of hope?

I'm out of space on my walls. Even the room between the pieces is taken. Anything in-between them will off-kilter the eye path for everything else. Maybe I should paint it over? Maybe start over with something in color. Maybe a black background. Can do a cosmos thing then. So, any light I use would accentuate the highlights. Candlelight on the galaxy? That might be something. No. Stop. No fantasies about staying here. That sounded like me mentally preparing to stay. Last thing I want to do.

Bad habits tend to find me on a roof. You'd think I'd learn, but prescription pain killers and whiskey make laying down the greatest thing on the planet. Especially when the temperature's just right on a clear night. Seriously, fame, fortune, rollercoasters; all frivolous nonsense when you can lay down on whiskey and painkillers. You sink into a hug.

Maybe that's it. Maybe it's not so much the psychic comfort but just the lack of guilt. Maybe that's what this combo does. Maybe I can just coast on prescription drugs if I sequence it out. Not to make it a habit, but a distant routine. Not like I'm in short supply. Engineer myself the satisfaction of having my shit together even if it's the furthest thing from together. Farthest? No, furthest. Farther's an actual distance while further is...I don't know, everything else.

I hear running water? Huh, why is my so-called "Dad" taking a bath at this hour?

Huh, why is my so-called "Dad" still asleep? I haven't been awake before eleven since high school. Impressive, seeing how I have never been awake before him. At least since I accomplished object permanence. More coal for that fire, I guess. I'll sleep at Jesse's tonight. Better to avoid whatever is going on. If he's not driving to work, I will.

"The fuck it so dead today?" Terrance asks me.

"Probably because people caught on that tea brewed inside a vacuum doesn't do anything."

"Raises the price ov' the bitch." I can never nail his liberal use of the word "bitch." He uses it as you would "shit," and "shit" as you would "fuck." He never made a move or passive sexual advance though, and thank god for that, because I would put my keys in my eyes if Terrance suggested we "shit."

"That it does." It doesn't take away from me liking the toasted coconut lavender oolong though. I should really take that home. It's cute they put employees' art on the walls, but all that does is let me see no one buy my abstract stencil of Nick Cave. Maybe it's how they get you to not turn in your notice. "Here, let us demonstrate how there's no place for your ambitions so you might as well not ask for time off." Clever devils. Hmm, I doubt the thought of that power play turned me on. Oh wait, I'm on my period. Wait. "Wait...ow." Ow.

"You 'kay?"

"...yeah" I say as I crumble into an unconscious heap on the rustic hardwood.

"When was your last pap smear?" a lady bored out of her mind asks me. The coat and stethoscope are a nice touch, but it wouldn't hurt to put a little oomph into asking about vagina cancer.

"Uh, never."

"Are you sexually active?"

"When available."

"Do you use contraceptives."

"Yup."

"Alcohol? Drugs?"

"Only when I'm sexually active." Nothing. I thought it was cute. She marks that down on my medical chart. Are we ever allowed to see that, or does it just get passed around to medical professionals? I also hate that my feet can't touch the floor on these tables. It's hard enough I'm wearing a big paper towel with no back. Do I have to feel like I'm in a highchair? Maybe that's how they keep you submissive? Since you feel so vulnerable, you revert back to your childhood, doing whatever a parental figure tells you.

"What kind of narcotics?"

"Whoa, 'narcotics.' Nothing I would call a narcotic. Bit of weed here or there. You know, marijuana." It feels weird to lie while also revealing I smoke pot.

"Do you know of any family history with cervical cancer? Cysts?"

"Um, cysts. My mother." Nothing. Not even eye contact.

"And what was her treatment."

"Uh, she didn't make it that far. She bit it from something else."

"Ah, well. I'm sorry to hear that, but I suggest you don't do the same. I'm ordering lab work as well as Percocet to help manage the pain." She finally makes eye contact while ripping the prescription. "Take this to the front desk and they'll schedule you for a follow-up. They remain this severe, we'll see if we can suppress your menstruation."

"'Suppress menstruation?'" "Mmm hmm."

"How?"

"There's a few treatments that can manage or stop periods. Continual use of oral birth control is the most common." She is blowing my mind right now.

"And that works?"

"We'll see what the lab work says. But low-dose birth control oral contraceptive can alleviate symptoms. I do it."

"Wait, you? Why?"

"I can't call in sick because lights give me migraines a few days out of the month. Nor do I normally want migraines."

"Sounds unfair. What about nature or punishment for some lady eating an apple or something?"

"By that token, half the country would have a hard time reading or driving."

"…." I don't get—Oh, she's motioning to her glasses. "Ah, glasses. Went over my head there. And it's safe?"

"With a moderately healthy lifestyle, it's safe in moderation and under doctor supervision."

"What about an unhealthy lifestyle?"

"Liver damage, hypertension, heart disease. All the symptoms of a poor lifestyle, just amplified."

"Huh…thank you."

"You're welcome." That's the exit of a woman that doesn't worry about cramps.

I look down at my ticket for more ambition robbing hugs. Oh my god this hurts. Huh, I can read every letter in her signature. I might be holding the first legible prescription ever signed. "Silverstein."

———

I wonder if the person who schedules your lab work uses that information to give you a backstory. They sit behind glass all day and listen to soap operas from the waiting room. That has to rub off at least a little, right? If they see a prescription for chlamydia medication from the wife of the mayor, do they immediately start gossiping about an affair. "Well, the Mayor's a patient and he doesn't need chlamydia pills." Yeah, I bet they do. How can they not? On the way out, it's weird to see more than one parka on the coat rack. I'm wearing my work polo-shirt and the walk from the parking lot made me sweat.

———

I like the waiting areas at pharmacies. They're like the DMV; no one can get out of them. You could be a tech millionaire, a traffic cop or a rodeo clown, you have to sit in a janky linoleum clearing in a convenience store. I suppose you could shop but that throws a wet blanket on my equalizer theory.

What in god's name is a bear doing in here? Why in the hell is no one paying attention to the bear in a crappy retail store? And why the fuck is the bear getting into the self-check out, wearing a belt with pockets and carrying a basket filled with graham crackers?

"Kimberly!" the pharmacist yells.

"Do you see the bear?" I yelp and point.

She didn't see the bear. Maybe that's a symptom of cervical cancer? I knock back a Perc and chew it. It tastes like how I would imagine brass polish would taste, but I don't have water with me and I kind of dig the feeling of a numb mouth. I'll also be home before it really kicks in, so driving under an influence isn't really a—

"Kim, do I have a car?" George asks. I'm home. On a stool in the kitchen. I'm apparently eating cereal. How did that happen? Am I still chewing the Percocet? No, that's cereal. I do not like the sensation of cereal just appearing in your mouth. Is this the work of the second pill? No, can't be. I don't feel anything. Well, I'm not numb, so I don't feel not feeling anything. Wait, did George ask if—"Hey, Kim! Do I have a—"

"Car, yeah, I heard you."

"Oh great. Is it here?" He sounds devoid of sarcasm. Maybe I am high?

"Uh, yeah. I used it for work. It's in the driveway." He walks away mid-sentence.

"The blue one?" What the fuck?

"Hey, can I crash over your place tonight?" I ask Jesse over the phone.

"Yeah. Pops on the road? I can come over there," she proposes.

"No, no, George's here, I just need to get out of here."

"What's up? You okay?"

"Eh, he's weird, I'm feeling weird, and the cramps this time around are freakin' weird."

"Should I plug in the heating pad?"

REALITY SQUALL | 119

"Eh, maybe not, the vice clamp that usually crushes my organs is white hot for some fucking reason."

"Jesus, I'll dim the lights while I'm at it. Doors open."

"Thanks. See you in ten."

I lower the phone from my ear and hear Jesse say "Word" before I end the call. Shit, I'm already packed, might as well take that. I might not even come back. Am I supposed to? Whoever the hell my Dad is supposed to be couldn't even recognize his car. You know what? I'm overreacting. My hormones are all out of whack and that sourness is leading me to goofy assumptions. Plus, I feel like I ate a plugged-in blender. That's gonna warp my perception. He's been trying to be healthier lately and I didn't notice the gradual weight loss. I thought I saw a bear in a pharmacy today. Didn't get a news alert about that. And in hindsight, a bear would really fucking dig graham crackers. I'll sleep it off. I'll drown out this painful fog with a medicated fog and be as fresh as a daisy in a couple days.

I cram my sketchbook and new perception in my bag. I should tell my Dad I'm out for the night. I'll let a clearer head not assume he's a pod-person tomorrow. I hear the running water again. I'll let him know before he hops in the shower or bath. That's a heavy rush of water, so I guess bath. I knock on the wall near his open bedroom door before I look inside.

"Hey, honey. You good?" George says while putting his skin on a coat hanger. There's a large slit in the back that lets him slide into it like footy pajamas. He's pleasant enough, as the skeleton wrapped in parched muscle looks at me. His mustache remains on his skin along with his deflated penis. Even though I'm talking to a seemingly fine yet skinless version of my father, the penis thing is going to haunt me.

"Yeah...I'm fine. You?" What am I looking at?

"Yep, just getting ready for bed. You heading out for the night?"

"Uh, yeah, staying over Jesse's for the night if that's okay." It's just all shriveled and lost in pubes.

"Of course. Just let me know your plans in the morning."

"Sure...dad."

"Hey, and uh, when did we get this, um, couch?"

He was referring to the bed. He didn't know what a bed was. Hallucinations are one thing, but people you know saying crazy-ass shit is another. I could write off the car thing as a Dad's attempt at scathing sarcasm, but being coy about skinning yourself alive is extreme.

Wait, how long have I been walking? I can see Jesse's house. She's on the porch with that boxed red wine I've vomited up a handful of times. This feels wrong. It's 8:47. I left a little after eight. How's this possible?

I keep marching, but keep my eyes glued to Jesse. She doesn't get closer, or I don't. I don't know how to describe it. I don't have a mile marker to gauge what's happening. There's a mailbox about fifteen feet behind me. Alright, let's try this. I run to the mailbox. Now look at Jesse. Alight, not too different but it looks like it's fifteen feet further away. Or is it farther? It doesn't matter. I pat the plain Jane mailbox for good luck only to find out it's fiberglass. Well, not only do my insides want me to crumble into myself and explode like the house from *Poltergeist,* but now I'm itchy. Here we go.

I won't look away from Jesse as I walk forward. Okay, I get about fifteen feet closer and that's it. She stays stuck in the distance, yet my feet keep pumping. I look to the house to my immediate right. I'm passing it. I look back at Jesse. She hasn't move and now the house has reset to where I was. It's like a trick of the mind. Stuff shifts just outside of my peripheral vision and between blinks. I stop walking after what must be six minutes. I turn around. The mailbox. It's fifteen feet behind me. It's fifteen feet behind me and my arm fucking itches. I have no idea why, but I try to fake physics out. I mock-turn toward the mailbox and then juke myself toward Jesse. I will fucking get there. I will vomit that shitty red wine out of spite, I swear.

Nothing. Jesse and her house stay that far away. Fixed at a distance, I cannot get any closer. Well, shit. Guess I'll walk back home. Walking back, I see that the light in George's room is still on. He's usually asleep by nine, but he wasn't awake at eleven this morning. Oh yeah, he can also crawl out of his own skin and hang it on his door like a cheap suit. I don't make a decision, my body just does it for me. I keep walking. Passed my father's house. I don't know who's in there, but it's not my home. It's never been my home. Never felt like it. It's just a place I sleep.

I do the thing I do when I don't know what to do. I bought a mickey of whiskey. Or do you call it rye when you buy it as a mickey? I'm not sure of the difference, but I feel like a short plastic bottle of whiskey should be referred to as rye. For a society that propagates "drink responsibly", they keep manufacturing these cheap, easy-to-conceal bottles of booze. Maybe that's how they can exploit the rich and the poor? Whiskey and rye. Glass and plastic.

It's weird that drinking cheap whiskey makes me think of my mom. Just the smell of it. I miss her. I miss her more than she'd believe. She was somehow a buddy and a mother. She'd saw her own arm off if it would help me with any lot in life. Maybe that's why this weight hangs on me. I can't help but think I had a hand in what happened when it came to the "buddy" portion of our relationship. It was just hard to see her as a mother afterwards. We were only allowed to spend so much time together and I made her feel like it was a choir. I was afraid, but even at that age, I knew what it was doing. I mean, she gravitated toward her vices, but me being a little asshole probably got her running to said vices. She just wanted to spend time together and I exploited that. For what? I don't know. I wanted to see her, too, it was just hard to see her. Shit. Hormones. I'm terrible. Yeah, sure, I'll blame this on hormones. Maybe this is her inherited revenge.

Time to put my whiskey and painkiller theory to the test. On a park bench on a clear night, let's see if I can clock in five to eight hours. The weather's perfect for it and there isn't a shady vagrant in sight. Wait, was that a vagrant? I hope it wasn't. Well, maybe I hope it was. I don't want to have a night terror. They seem horrific. I've only ever heard stories and I know I'm genetically predisposed. Can sleep paralysis be passed down? I don't see why not? I'm starting to hit the buoy markers of what to expect. Holy shit, I don't want to see anything. I'm not opening my eyes. That's how it starts, right? You acknowledge night terrors and, bam, a three-dimensional shadow stares at you while you're paralyzed? Screaming into your face with all the shrieking sounds of Hell? No. Please. I'm not opening my eyes. I feel like I conjured one. He's there, isn't he? Or a demon cat on my chest? I'm not opening my eyes. I don't even want to take the chance.

My eyes open. The sky is a pale blue as the sun gets ready to rise. Man, I drank that whole bottle. I successfully avoided something I don't even know I should be worried about. I feel wrung out. I doubt dehydrating yourself on a stomach full of opioids and booze is the cure for period cramps, but I don't feel them. The fog, with the help of the blurry streetlights, makes this park a hell of a dreamscape. Always liked these times of the day. When the lights are still on but it's still bright enough to see. I guess I should be going but where am I going?

"Why the shit are you in today?" Terrance asks accordingly.

"I'm hung over and lavender-whatever-bullshit helps." Plus, sitting on this cool Persian marble has a soothing sensation going for it.

"More reason not to be in this fuck."

"Eh, not like I'm disturbing the peace," I say to the vacant artisanal tea shop.

"Hey, you been noticin' strange fucks lately?" Terrance asks after I almost forget about my skin suit shedding ascendent.

"'Fucks' a noun or a verb?"

"Both."

I'm not even sure why I'd lie but "....no more than usual."

"Eh, awight," Terrance mumbles away, leaving room for me to intervene. I don't.

"Well...," jumping off the countertop "I'm getting lunch. You want anything?"

"I don't know. Something. Where you going?"

"I might see how much buffet cornbread and melon I can cram down."

"Ugh, come on, that bitch place?"

"Kind of want to sit and sketch and eat as I please."

"Food court mall buffets, man. It's sketchy enough for that."

"Har, har, har, I'll getchya a hotdog or somethin'."

"Thanks, man."

It's insane to me that buffets have cloth napkins. We're at a buffet; one in a mall food court. We left our dignity with the hostess. Just have a paper towel roll on the table. Now, a glutton will tell you to load up on protein first and then hit up the starches, but when you have a particular penchant for the simplest of carbohydrates, the order of operations isn't an issue. Plus, cornbread dipped in water-drowned chicken and stars is the best-possible menu item.

I can't remember the last time I sketched in a restaurant. I forgot how productive I can be in a setting like this. Maybe the lack of a waiter helps. And since it's an odd lunch hour whilst also being a mall buffet, it's pretty damn quiet. It's vacant enough for me to notice the new "licensed trucker" section. What the fuck? When was that added? It's been a while since I've step foot in here but we're in a suburban neighborhood. What truckers are coming through here? Maybe a new inter-state's in development and they're preparing this place to be a truck stop? Might as well, malls are on their way out. It's the inevitability of the corporate power structure. Soon, all land-scapes will just be mega-warehouse supply chains and roads to transport said supplies. Truckers got to eat and shit- "what the fuck? What the actual fuck?" It was loud the first time I blurted out and just as loud the second. "What the fuck." That one is a bit more couth.

That looks way too much like her to be a coincidence. But she's younger? Exactly like how I remember her. No, it can't

be. But it is. Did she fake her own death? Dad and I identi-
fied the body? My god that body. It took me years to not see
it every time I closed my eyes. What am I doing? I feel like a
spy with a head injury. What are the chances she'd also be a
trucker, though? Shit, head down. She's crossing the rope.

My nose points to my book but my eyes stay on her. She's
coming this way. Please don't see me. Just grab whatever you
want from the buffet and get back outside of my field of vision.
What am I doing? This is absolutely ridiculous. That is in no
way my mother. Oh my god, it's my mother. That smell. That
stale yet somehow pleasant aroma of pancake batter. Sweet-
ness swaddled in a blanket of starch Her smell. It cuts through
my brain and throttles my memories. It's a wave of nostalgia
that adds a teardrop to my open sketch book. I don't know
what to do. What do I do? Maybe my dad taking off his skin
wasn't a hallucination? If that could happen, why couldn't that
be her? It's impossible to know the possible once the impossible becomes possible, right? Right?!

Once she leaves her booth, I scuttle to her seat. I don't
know what I'm going to find. I'm not even sure if I can reclaim
the smell. Looking down at her war zone of empty plates, I
pretty much verify that she's my mother. No one on earth uses
that much butter. Not even for a tall stack of pancakes. What
the hell? Does this trucker area lead to a convenience store?
And that store exits to a gas station? When did that happen?
Hearing the bathroom door open makes me panic. The first
bad idea I abandon is hurdling over the stanchions. I should
avoid toppling into a tangled nest of retractable belts. There's
only one other option. I scamper into the magically-conjured
convenience store.

This isn't new. It can't be. Grime lives on every corner and
if the wire racks used to white, they aren't anymore. The smell
alone is stale and I'm sure there's discontinued candy fossiliz-
ing below the counter. That is also the withdrawn and hopeless slouch of a lifelong gas station employee. The same can
be said for the exterior. That parking lot isn't a part of this
mall. I walk up to the glass door. It's a legit truck stop. A field
of pavement with parked semi-trucks peppered around even

fewer cars. Surrounding the lot is a forest thicker than anything within a twenty-mile radius of this neighborhood.

There it is. That's it. Watching her step into that and drive
off was a trademark of my childhood. That goldfinch-yellow
license plate fading into that musty sea foam blue detail of
the truck. Shit. That's it. Oh god, this is almost too much. I
don't think the brain is designed for this level of nostalgia.
Road trips. Mom. Dad. Drums. I love them so much. It's way
too much. What am I supposed to do? This can't be real. My
feet want me to sprint as hard and as fast as I can into Mom's
truck. Not even to look at it but to caress it. Smell it. Hear it
ring again when I knock on its hood. I want to squeeze it so
hard my arms break. I practically want to eat. Where is she?
I want to cry in her arms. This can't be good for my psyche.
What is this?

Maybe this is some kind of acid-less acid flashback. But if
that were the case, how can I be somewhere I've never been?
Maybe I'm manifesting a composite from a mishmash of
half-remembered truck stops? I see myself in the mirror of
the sunglass rack. She's never seen this look. A head-shaved
adult with a wayward punk black aesthetic. Maybe a hat will
seal the deal?

I look back toward her. She's paying at the cashier. Passed
her, the buffet, the polo shirt, the food court and the sausage
and cheese cart, Terrance awaits a hotdog. Sorry, dude. The
universe and/or mental disorder is calling.

███

What the hell am I doing? Why would she pick me up?
Why would she pick anyone up with how well her last hitchhiker went? She might have had more. That's just the meet-
cute story you tell your kid. Dad had a flat and was trying to
get to a gas station. Mom picked him up and after a minute,
BAM, love. She had a jack in her truck but didn't say anything
because she wanted to spend more time with Dad? She even
avoided passing gas stations. For what? Dad? Please, that's too
romantic. The Hallmark Channel would scoff at that. Mom
was into that shit though. What the hell am I talking about? I

was nine. I'm making up what kind of woman she was. Well, maybe this is my chance to actually know. Maybe get dirt on what really happened but skip the sex stuff. Don't need or want to hear that. You know, if this is real which it's not.

I try not to look too desperate by getting some time in contact juggling. It's been a while so I'm rusty. It was purchased while I was high out of my gourd at a music festival. This thing has seen better days. I've dropped it more times than I can count. Got to say, it does calm the nerves.

I take a pill. All they do is dull the pain instead of relieve it. I can still feel the cramps; they're just further away. Maybe that's what's going on. One too many pain-killed nights. Maybe that has diluted my synapses into seeing a tangentially stitched together reality. I've become so distant from my dad, my mind's interrupting him as an imposter. This might be an early sign of Capgras Syndrome. Maybe my mom had a dash of that as well? I have to say, this experience puts my childhood in a new light. If this gets worse, who knows what I'm capable of.

Here she comes. I put out my thumb. I'm not even sure if she saw me. Well, that was interesting. I guess I should try to teleport back to the mall. At least I got a hat out of this endeav—"You okay with cats?" a grandmotherly voice hits my back. "...and heading North?" I guess that was for me.

"Hm?" I turn to a white hatchback, oblivious to her question.

"Sorry, I saw your thumb up and thought you were looking for a ride."

"Me?" In the act of motioning to myself, I drop my glass ball.

"Yes, if you still want one?" she asks.

I stand up straight, with sphere in hand, and look to the truck stop. It's as sterile and depressing as you can get. Compared to the open road on a clear day, the walk through a food court buffet doesn't even have an ironic appeal. I stare down at the horizon. I don't know where I am, I have no idea how this is possible, and I can't imagine it'll end well. One thing's for sure, it'll be better than an unpaid internship.

"Thank god for you. It's a long trek and keeping her in the cat carrier for hours on end seems cruel," Samantha compliments. Behind the wheel of her sports utility vehicle, she knows how to drive in comfort. Vanilla chai scents are clipped onto the vents and she's in a matching pastel jumpsuit. There's a Doc Brown thing going on as I can't tell if she looks good for eighty or rough for forty. Either way, I like her cat.

"How's she in the car without the carrier?"

"Troublemaker. She's partial to the space under the brakes."

"Can't have that," I say as I rub this little tub of fluff's belly. It's always depressing when you see an overweight dog, but fat cats are downright adorable. And they wear the weight well. They seem happier. I guess within reason, if their organs are healthy and they're content, why should anyone care? "I love it when cats do this." She curls around my hand with gentle claws and her nibbling tickles my fingers.

"Powerfully fetching, right?"

"Happy cat," I can't help but squeak.

"Should have met her when she was kitten?"

"Extra adorbs?"

"Quite the opposite. She'd do that, but was lousy at measuring the amount of force behind her claws. My hands were riddled with scratches for a couple years."

"Oof. And the sting of cat scratches…"

"Knitting was arduous for a while." Of course she knits.

"How'd you train it out of this bundle?" I ask as I roll the furry gal over.

"I didn't."

"So, what'd you do?"

"Nothing. She figured it out. I wasn't going to stop petting her."

"I mean, how could you?" This little ragamuffin's purring.

———

Our conversations don't evolve passed petting cats. Honestly, it's just as profound as our life stories or where we're going. The human experience is pretty banal if you ask me. From tragic to privileged. It's been done and will continue to repeat until extinction. Now, eleven million years ago, nature forged a four-legged killing machine the size of a go-cart in North Africa. That thing bounced around Africa and Asia until some asshole from Europe brought it to North America. They had to because they were awesome at killing pests on boats. Well, that murderer hopped off and started eviscerating the wildlife in the new world. Flash forward four-hundred years and they're taking naps on laptops and dominating the internet. They won natural and unnatural selection. Even with the teleportation, I can't top that.

"Whoa, hey, sorry, but could you drop me off there—" I ask to a passing disgusting tavern. Her semi is pulling into the parking lot. What are the chances of that?

"I have to turn around but I certainly can," Samantha answers.

"If you don't mind?"

"I certainly don't," Samantha proclaims as she slows down into the open space of the median.

"Thank you again. That was nothing but lovely," I say to Samantha as I step out of the passenger's side door.

"My pleasure and safe travels."

"You, too." Her cat is nestled in some towels on the front seat. I guess she's going to try to avoid the cat carrier. "Bye, Anita," I say as I scratch her head. She leans her head into my hand and that will never not release serotonin. Samantha drives off. My instincts tell me to survey the exterior of this dim roadside pub, but her truck is parking into its space. The brake lights are still on, but I panic. I guess my body responds with "flight," because I scurry into the pub as if my mother is a prehistoric predator.

Wow, I thought it was dilapidated on the outside. A puke green sign, that's probably supposed to glow, reads "Pic-A-Lilli's." In an attempt to look cavalier, I cozy up to the bar. It's hard to look cool when your mind's propagated with doubt. I'm sure the bartender's not going to mind as he stares into the middle space. He looks like a Rockwell painting. I'll never look that natural leaning against a freestanding chest fridge.

REALITY SQUALL | 129

It's vintage but I don't think it's by design. It seems impossible that this place used to be new.

I give the bartender a little wave. Hopefully his peripheral vision can catch it. Wow, he's off somewhere far away. I lean over the bar and try again. Nothing. I could use some liquid edge filers. My eyes volley between the door and the liquor. It's not too crazy in here so maybe this is his mental siesta before the midnight crowd. I'll let him finish his ruminating while I dryly drink in the surroundings.

The screeching of my stool as I sit back down gets the bartender's attention. "Hi," he throws my way.

"Hi, how's it going?"

"Fine. What can I get you?" he asks as he leans both hands on the bar. He looks exhausted. Other than "go to bed", I feel bad asking him to do anything.

"Um, whiskey."

"Brand?" he asks with his head hanging toward the ground.

"Something weird."

He looks up.

"Okay," he says as he walks off. He seems to have trouble finding anything behind the bar, let alone something weird. He does find a jug of something clear that he uncorks and sniffs. He doesn't reel back from the stench, but he does breathe through his mouth as he puts it back. He seemingly gives up on finding something weird when he finds his first bottle of whiskey. Someone walks in but it isn't her.

How was that burrito?" the bartender asks. For someone I've never met, he sure recognizes me.

"Burrito?"

"This morning? You and Jamie or whatever" he mutters away.

Jamie? Jamie. "Holy shit!" The burst of vulgarity is a combo of aligning coincidences and the sight of a fucking monster playing cards. It's sitting quietly at its own booth. Why is no one baffled by the tree man? I look at my bartender. "Do you see that?"

He looks over at the creature and gets back to me. He acts like I asked him to look at a pigeon. He shrugs. "Need anything else?"

"Bathroom?" The words just ooze out of my mouth.

He motions behind me, and I see the graffiti'd bathroom stick figures. "Thanks."

Fucking timed lights. I'm trying to cry here. I'm already losing my mind, I don't need a strobe light to enhance the experience. This was a bad idea. I don't even know what state I'm in and I'm scribbling on the bathroom wall of a truck stop bar. My knuckles hurt and I'm not even sure why. I should check into a hospital. I need clinical help. That's what I'm going to do. I'm going to call an ambulance and drink as much as possible before they get here. I'll knock back half of my painkillers to seal the deal. A podunk watering hole like this, it'd take paramedics a minute to get here. I could get to a point that'd justify medical attention. Then I won't feel guilty about the physical aid for a mental issue.

I'm a mess. I wash my face in the sink until my fingertips prune. I can't remember my last glass of water, but I cry out whatever hydration I had left. I drink water right from the faucet. The little bit of mirror behind the ratty bumper stickers shows me my eyes. They're bloodshot and tired. I drink as much water from the sink as my stomach will allow. It might keep me alive for the amount of self-destruction I'm about to commit. Alright, here we go. Literal cry for help coming up.

I walk out of the bathroom and my plans immediately evaporate. There she is.

10

"KIM," CARL REITERATES.

"As in Kimberly?" Jamie continues.

"I don't know, maybe." Carl drifts his attention to Twigs. "This is easy. What is this?" Carl asks while exhaling the pipe weed.

"Owlbranch and skullcap. Some lavender as well to percolate the lingering flavor," Twigs answers as he accepts the pipe.

Jamie stares at Anita with whiskey in hand. She hasn't noticed Jamie as she finds her usual seat at the bar. Jamie studies Anita while the booze stings her senses.

"I get the lavender," Carl comments.

"Oh, it's absolutely capital. I have yet to indulge in the that particular *Lamiaceae*," Twigs informs as it empties the ash in the nape of its neck. Its mechanical innards hiss in a red glow as it digests the ash.

"Really? Carl asks.

"I have not sojourned to an earth that nurtured its germination."

The way she sits in a chair. How she rests her left hand on the rim of her glass. What her hair color actually is under the dye and what her style would transform into after a decade. Her mind completes its computation and Jamie comes to a conclusion. "Oh shit...oh shit...oh shit..." Jamie hyperventilates as she peels back the mystery that is Anita.

"You okay?" Carl asks.

Finding the liquor in her hand, Jamie places the shot glass down. "Same hair. Brown eyes."

"Who?" Carl looks over to whom he knows as Kim, but Jamie knew as Anita.

"Kim? Yeah. Okay. What about her?"

"Anita, she said her name was Anita."

"Well, she told me Kim, but who the hell knows these days."

"Oh god...jesus. It's Kimmy. That's Kimmy."

"Kimmy, your kid, Kimmy?

"That's her. That's her."

"Kimmy's seven."

"And that guy has seven arms," Jamie moans while pointing to the Arms.

"Chat chat," Arms chirps.

"Look where we are! You don't think that could be Kimmy?" Vocalizing her theory only solidifies it.

Carl looks back over to Arms. "Chat chat," Arms says with a seven-shouldered shrug.

"I'm still not used to you," Carl peeps.

"Chat."

"Don't I know it." Carl looks over at Twigs. "Sorry, uh, twig guy?"

"Pardon?" Twigs answers while Embers raises attention to the predicament.

"Could that be Jamie's seven-year-old daughter?" Carl points over to Anita as Twigs and Embers look on without moving their neck.

"Everything that can and cannot has, is, will and won't happen. That *could* be Jamie's daughter." Twigs motions to an armless woman with four legs and eight pitch black eyes.

"Ugh, fine, but could that be her daughter from her reality, from their future?"

"Nothing isn't, so yes. Everything's experience is dictated by their quantum world line, so it's as likely as is it isn't."

"It's amazing how much I don't understand what you're talking about."

"Quantum fields ensure that matter remains in feasible parameters while in flux—"

"Dumber please."

"While everything's screwy, your matter's making sure you don't end up in a wall or in an uninhabited atmosphere," Embers explains.

"I was wondering why I was alive," Carl says.

"That doesn't preclude the dangers, however."

"But on a molecular level, Jamie or her daughter could consider their presence…vital," Twigs concludes.

"Wait…really?" Jamie chimes in.

"Possibly. There are precisely infinite variables," Embers begrudgingly divulges.

"Carl takes a moment to comprehend that answer. "….Alright, Jamie. Look at me." An imploding Jamie's head turns to Carl but her eyes lack focus. "If it is, what do you want to do about it?"

Jamie's eyes find their focus. She looks at Carl. "I…um…"

"Do you want to talk to her?"

"Um, I have. It, ah, it didn't go well."

"But do you want to talk to her, as her mother?"

"Eh…," is all that can leave her mouth. Her head wobbles with indecision, but Carl reads more nods than shakes.

"Okay. It's okay. You've got this."

"I…I don't know if I can."

"Jamie, you got me on your couch when I was fine drinking myself to death. Let's go do something for you."

Jamie cringes and throws her hands up in submission. "Who cares with universes smashing into each other and infinity and whatever the hell all…?" Jamie continuously motions to the bar, feigning a desperate chuckle.

"Yeah? What does that have to do with you and your daughter?" Carl interrupts, challenging Jamie's theatrics.

Bitter, Jamie stares back at Carl with an expression that would normally portend homicide. Carl throws his hands up as an innocent simper flops across his cheeks. Jamie's bravado folds "Ugh…Jesus."

"Right the fuck on!" Carl stands up and offers Jamie his hand. She disparagingly looks at her compatriots. Their support is brimming, barring Frederick's confusion. She stands.

With eye contact affixed to Carl's, Jamie marches past him, away from Anita. "Um, she's—" Jamie enters the bathroom and slams the door loud enough to momentarily hush the bar. "...well." Carl sits back down. He looks to Twigs. "Fifth dimensional, huh?"

"Indeed," Twigs answers.

"What's that like?"

"Not too dissimilar from you. I just experience all of my consciousness' possibilities at once. Past and future."

"Oh, are there sixth dimensional folks?"

"There are."

"What do they experience?"

"Every consciousness at once."

"Trippy."

"Quite."

Most of Jamie's explosive vomit enters the toilet bowl. The remainder leaves a trail, starting from the door. Hoping confidence will quell the nausea, Jamie attempts to stand. "Alright." She wipes the residual puke from her lips. "Alright," she utters along with a deep breath. "Here we g—" She falls back down. Folding onto her knees, she vomits a myriad of colors and textures. She hugs the bowl. The stench alone provokes more heaving, invoking a more rancid stench, causing more vomit. If Jamie had more control of her actions, she would consider flushing. The contents touch the rim of the toilet. Whatever partially-digested food, booze and pills were inside Jamie is now outside.

With tear-stained eyes and a pounding heart, Jamie strikes euphoria. No longer nauseous, she closes her eyes and rotates her tense jaw.

"Uh huh....uh huh." Jamie's tongue surveys her mouth. Bile slick gristle hides between her lips and teeth. Whatever moisture is left in her mouth is used to spit out the half-digested morsels. She spits again for good measure and finally flushes. She flushes again to get the floating bits of fast food and stringy phlegm. It takes a second, but the rank air smells less of vomit and rot. Jamie breathes deeply and rests her head

REALITY SQUALL | 135

on the seat of the toilet. It's cool and satisfying. Her skin feels as if it fuses with the porcelain.

In that moment of quiet reprieve, Jamie keeps her eyes closed and embraces the sensation of not gagging. When she opens her eyes, she finds a crude sketch of Twigs on the bathroom wall. The question has been answered by dozens and dozens of different inks and strokes. "Yes," "yup," "mmm hmm," "yep," "yeah," 'certainly" and "can't you?" are etched next to the sharpie question "can you see it?" Jamie raises her head and smirks at the image. "Heh. Wow. Today." Using the toilet as support, she gets to her feet.

Misery can be a safety blanket. The descent into depression is insufferable, but the impact can bear catharsis. Knowing there is nowhere else to plummet, the mind can rest in that melancholia. There is nothing to risk. You are at the bottom. Consequences are moot. This is where despair becomes addictive and self-sabotage becomes an option. The further the drop, the harsher the impact. Jamie has long feared that fall and has cultivated several counter measures to avoid the plunge. Time has transformed the whisper of experience into a scream. Jamie, right now, is using that momentum to slingshot her into uncharted hope.

"How you feeling?" Carl asks as Jamie closes the bathroom door.

"Like I just threw up a million bucks," Jamie answers.

"Listen, you don't have to do anything you don't want to."

"Then I wouldn't ever do anything."

Carl's eyelids flutter at the conviction. This is the Jamie that challenged Carl's demons. "Let's get over there."

As Jamie makes her way toward Anita's back, Carl pats her shoulder for support and branches off to his table. *Don't overthink. That lack of a plan is the plan. This is unprecedented, so there's nothing to plan for. Adapt. Cautious instincts.* Jamie does an anxious tap on the bar as she steps up beside Anita. *But how the hell do you start this conversation?*

"Hey, um, how goes it?" Jamie fiddles.

"Oh, sup," Anita forces.

"Mind if I...?" Jamie slides the adjacent stool back.

"Sure. I can't stop ya." Anita flippantly jests as she goes back to sketching in her book.

Trying to camouflage her nerves, Jamie sits on her stool and remembers to breathe. "So, What's shakin'?"

Anita doesn't look up. "Oh, nothing much I suppose. Still hitching."

Without an opening, Jamie uses her surroundings to pivot the conversation. "This Reality Squall is nuts, huh?" Jamie says while looking at the four-legged woman with spider eyes.

"Is that what you call it?" Anita trills with eyes on her drawing.

"I guess. I just thought it was me," Jamie says as she peeks over Anita's shoulder. Anita strategically covers her sketch with her elbow. Realizing she isn't leaving, Anita dramatically sighs as she turns to Jamie. "Yeah, so did I, but then I started going with the flow." Jamie believes she catches an image of an English Bulldog in her book.

Jamie reels back to avoid being caught. "You seem to be managing it...well. Better than me, anyway."

"I think I jumped on the bandwagon before the rest of the world. Got to look for some cool shit."

"Yeah? Did you find anything?"

Anita's eyes find Jamie before her face. "I don't know what you—"

Reminiscent of Count Orlok's glare, the thought that this could end with violence pricks Jamie. To reciprocate, she abandons tact.

"Kimmy?" Jamie asks just above a whisper.

Anita merely stares back. Eyes wide, witnessing a terrifying miracle.

"Kimberly?" Jamie reiterates in a soulful breath. Anita's teeth grind as she stares at her mother. Jamie reaches out to touch her daughter's shoulder, but her hand might as well be fire.

"Don't!"

"Oh, wow, it is you. It's me. It's okay. It's your—"

Anita rockets out of her chair. She backs away and coils as if she were in the vicinity of a cobra. "Don't...No!...no."

The bar turns still. The bustling activity of flesh, scale, fur, crystal, and light takes notice of the maternal plight.

"Best not intervene" Twigs comments to the conflicted Carl. Shifting his weight into his seat, Twigs felt the tension shift in the floorboards. Humbled by the interjection, Carl relaxes into his chair. He looks to his table of misfits. They warmly nod in solidarity, eyes away from Jamie's dispute.

Mortified, Anita looks to the room. Eyes of all shapes briefly glance at her. Despite the momentary attention, every millisecond clenches down on Anita's soul. A decade older and this would cause her an aneurysm. She looks to her mother. Pathetic. Everything she came looking for, she found after it was too late. Damage has been done. She might as well be looking into a mirror. Putrid and rotting, inside and out. Hope brought her to Jamie, but disgust makes her leave. Anita runs off into the bathroom.

"Kimberly!" Jamie exclaims. She turns to Carl and the rest of her table. "What just happ—"

"Don't think about it," Carl hollers across the bar.

"But—" Jamie tentatively stutters.

"Go!"

After a less-than-confidant nod, Jamie looks to the bathroom door. She jogs to it and grips onto the handle before the lock sets into the frame. Leaving a crack in the door, Jamie talks to a sliver of light.

"Listen, I totally understand if you don't want to see me. Believe me, I get it. Say the word, I'll leave. It's okay, I will. But if you would like to take this...bizarre opportunity to talk, I'll be seated at the booth with the tree guy and...," Jamie realizes the harsh fluorescence has been replaced by something more natural. A crisp daylight hue illuminates her chest. "Kimb-Anita?"

Jamie opens the door to her apartment.

"The fuck, and who are—" A second Jamie barks while looking at Jamie from their own apartment. The second Jamie has an egg sandwich in her hand. She's closing her front door but freezes at the sight of a familiar intruder. She stands dumbfounded, looking at her future self. Post-shower, she peers toward her doppelgänger in a robe and wet hair. Jamie closes the bathroom door behind her.

"Whoa, shit uh, did a woman just run through here?"

Alternate Jamie points to the front door.

"Thanks," Jamie remarks as she makes her way through the kitchen.

"Ahhhhhh....dang." A cool gust of wind strikes Jamie's face. Even though this door used to lead to an apartment hallway, she is now outside. In the span of twelve seconds, Jamie's eyes had to adjust from a dimly lit bar, a sunny apartment, and now a night exterior. She keeps her hand pressed against the door as her eyes adjust. It's black. "Come on. Come on, come on, come on." A stale sea breeze above the concrete gives Jamie a hint of her location. Her iris regains some acuity and a raging sky of celestial bodies comes into focus. The shapes under the star swollen heavens find definition. Trucks. Rows of semi-trucks in a battered parking lot. "There you!" Anita is in the distance. Seeing Jamie, she barrels onward past the lanes upon lanes of trucks.

Jamie pursues her temporally-distant daughter. Scouring in-between the trailers, she finds a groaning Carl leaning against a tire. He's staring into the sky, mouth agape, and a bottle loosely gripped in a limp hand. His body composition is radically different. The girth in his shoulders has moved to his waistline but his cheeks are gaunt under vacant eyes. It's hard to gauge his age. The thought that this may not be the past hisses through Jamie's mind. Carl's head flops in Jamie's direction. His frail body moves with soulless autonomy.

"Jamie?" he asks.

"I, uh—" The clang of a metal door echoes through the lot. "Ani-Kimberly!" Jamie hollers. She's walked this lot thousands of times and has heard that door close just as many. She sprints away, leaving the inebriated heap to wallow. Finding the rusted door, Jamie rams her shoulder against it and turns the knob. The extra force only hardens the impact.

Jamie lands on the ceiling of a rustic coffee shop. "Agh, mother...fucker!" Jamie blurts.

"How are they doing that?" a child's voice asks.

"Sorry. Sorry," Jamie apologizes. Looking up, she finds the child. Gravity is inverted but only for Jamie. Homey wood furnishings and a red and white picnic color scheme remain above her as Jamie gets to her feet. She stays crouched down to help mitigate her vertigo along with not headbutting a waiter.

The coffee shop patrons look up at Jamie and their eyes and mouths have switched positions on their faces.

"Whoa, shit," the waiter yelps, noticing Jamie's disfigured face. Still disoriented, Jamie lowers herself to her hands and knees.

Jamie makes eye contact with the curious toddler. The sight of a mismatched face forces the toddler to bury her face in her mother's shirt. Her mother covers her face and looks on in terror at the outcast of physics and anatomy.

"That way, Jamie." Twigs, with the universe's appropriate alterations, plays a game of solitaire on a corner table.

"Oh, Jesus. Hey," Jamie responds.

"She went through there." Twigs motions to the front door.

"Thanks." The windowpane shows the overcast main street of a rural town. Backward-faced shoppers, dressed for autumn, peruse through artisanal bakeries and hobby shops. It's horrifying. Jamie crawls to the front door. If she walks through it and is not transported to Anita's location, when will she stop falling upwards? The troposphere? Outside of this earth's orbit? Or maybe she'll just collide into a streetlamp or airplane? Either way, she'll be dead. That provides some morbid comfort. She guides her hands up the frame of the door and grips onto the handle.

"Alright, here we go," Jamie barks to herself in an attempt to inflate her confidence. She repeats some quick shallow breaths before a large gulp of air.

"Safe travels," Twigs says.

Holding her breath, Jamie turns the upside doorknob and leaps outside.

The air pushes out of her lungs on impact, but the hard floor below her gives Jamie some relief. "Uh, sweet. Got it. Good," Jamie wheezes with a labored exhale. Determined to stand, she overrides her lung's absence of breath and stands up. Like a boxer at the count of eight, she stumbles from a light head. She finds a wall for support. Air returns to her body and the soles of her feet find the floor. Then, terror.

A cacophony of snarls and barks bombard her from all directions. They pierce her ears, paralyzing Jamie with a crackling yap. Frozen in place, Jamie focuses on a drain embedded in the concrete floor. Her eyes gradually drift to find the bottom of a fence. She visually works her way up, finding aggressive fangs. Wincing from the sight of an angry dog, Jamie coils away. The jolt brings awareness, and she finds herself inside a dog shelter. Seeing how two humans magically exited a storage closet brought calamity inside the shelter. Looking to the German Shepherd lunging toward her, Jamie covers her ears. Jamie's vision shrinks to the immediate. Catatonic by the sound, she looks to anywhere and everywhere for some kind of reprieve. She finds it.

A recognizable fold on meek paws shivers in its pen. A puppy named Bob huddles in the corner. Jamie's phobia is pulverized by warmth.

"Hey...," Jamie coos to the frightened pup. "It's okay, buddy." Jamie kneels down to his pen. "Bob? Bob. It's okay." Shy and timid, Bob's body stays facing the corner but his eyes peak toward Jamie. "It's okay. It's okay, little buddy. I know, they're loud." Bob turns to Jamie. "Come here. It's okay." Leaning against the cage, Jamie encourages the little bulldog. "I know. It's rough, but I got good news." Bob waddles closer to Jamie. "Guess what? Soon, very soon, you're going to get out of here." Meek from a world so big and impossible, Bob writhes in the middle of his pen in uncertainty. "I know. Me, too. They're scary, but you'll get a home soon. Mmm hmm, yup, you are. Away from all this with your own comfy bed you won't sleep in because you like the couch and a dog bowl you'll flip over every morning. And the folks you'll live with? Oh man, they might not have their shit together, but the one thing they all agree on is how much they love you. Hang in there little buddy. Okay? And see you soon."

Jamie almost forgot her predicament. Standing up, she finds Anita looking back at her at the end of the hall of cages. Repulsed by her own sentimentality, Anita steps back.

Jamie coos once more but toward a human.

"Hey..."

Anita shakes her head as she backpedals.

"It's okay. Seriously..."

She doesn't run but marches away, disappointed by her own vulnerability.

Jamie lowers her head from the setback but sees the lack of sprint as a small victory. "I'll see you soon little buddy. Stay brave." Jamie encourages Bob. She walks to the end of the hallway and Bob watches her.

When she turns the corner, Jamie isn't met with a door, but a lapse in physics. Her stride travels past the linear plane and wraps around the elements. Her vision gently echoes from the sterile halogen of the dog shelter to the peaceful glow of the morning sun. It's all so seamless. Jamie's senses euphorically transition to the warm light and the scent of dew. Jamie revolves upright from the ground into a field of wildflowers. She isn't perplexed by the maneuver as it felt as natural as drinking water.

Anita shares the space.

"Kimberly, Jesus Christ, Anita," Jamie calls out. Anita turns to Jamie, defeated in her posture. The chase has concluded. Not only did Jamie keep pace but she also followed her through time and space.

"Jamie? Oh my god, help me," Billy pleads. Mangled and confused, Billy limps toward Jamie at the edge of the meadow.

"What the? Billy?" asks Jamie.

Anita looks over at the injured man as he lurches his way toward them.

"Don't we know him?" Anita asks.

"Fellow trucker and also a douche," Jamie answers. It dawns on Jamie that that acknowledgment is a faint admission of their connection. "Looks like he's had a time."

"I mean, who hasn't?" Anita says.

"Please, oh my god, help..." Billy whimpers.

Ignoring Billy, the two look back at one another. In the smallest of steps toward Anita, Jamie falls forward and vanishes from this plane.

Flabbergasted by the sight, Billy stops in his hobble, "...me."

11

ALONE, JAMIE STANDS IN AN ABYSS. SHE LOOKS TO THE GROUND and sees a floor of obsidian. A dull reflection looks back at her. When she pivots her weight, violet wisps of color ripple away from her feet. Unlike walking on a puddle, the threads of purple disperse in three dimensions. Above and below Jamie's feet, they billow away from her body and diffuse into the darkness.

Ah, shit, Jamie hears her thought. She attempts to breathe but her lungs have nothing to inhale. Sheathed in a vacuum, Jamie panics inside a void of stasis. Trapped in an interstice of existence and nihility. Scrambling for the right to persist, Jamie attempts to raise her hands. It's as if she is moving in tar. The air around her fights her will. Every motion, voluntary and involuntary, is challenged. This place somehow contains a crushing gravity while also being a vacuum. Noxious heat as well as absolute zero sear Jamie's flesh. The imperious onslaught even bears down on her mind. The mere sensation of awareness pulls away from her. Clasping onto her identity, Jamie clings onto her being.

She drops to her hands and knees. Despite being numb, Jamie can feel her existence disintegrate. The smallest fragments of her body, down to her molecules, wither over to oblivion. She stays diligent on the precipice of doom. At first, her clamoring to carve her place in reality came from fear, then spite and then something she thought was a long-dead assumption. She *wants* to exist. Buried beneath all the dread and perceived

144 | J. KRAWCZYK

failures, desire flutters. Not just longing for pleasure but for agony. A hunger for the entire spectrum of sensation. Mourning, joy, depression, satisfaction, guilt, melancholy—all of it, every experience her mortal chassis can bear.

With Jamie's rebellion, nihilism summons its champion. In the eclipse below her,

An illuminated speck of blue sways toward her. The bioluminescent bulb dances in and out of her visibility, amplifying in intensity with each appearance. The gentle abstraction grabs Jamie's attention, hypnotizing her away from her corporeal drive. She shuts her eyes and grits her teeth to remain vigilant. She can see with her eyes closed. She can't scream in defiance, but she does defy this place by yearning to scream. Reliving the circumstances of how she ended up here fuels each roar. The memories usher in the flood of emotions that made them. Her nerves reciprocate to her demands. She may be silent, but she is screaming.

The void behind the light reveals a shape. Warped behind Jamie's rage, the shadow of a beast looms. Even in the black, the seriated mass of darkness is apparent. Lines. Rows and rows of lines is the first thing Jamie can distinguish. Teeth. Teeth as black as pitch and taller than Jamie. Resembling a deep-sea angler fish, the rows of translucent teeth unhinge from impossible jaws. Within its maw lies everything and nothing, an infinite spiral of charred ivory. The nightmare fractal envelopes eternity and Jamie loses her bearings. *Was there ever anything else? What is this? Words. Floating words. How would something know it's something? I am not anything. Just a glitch diluting back into nothing. That's all this is and ever will be.*

The light fades. Sound evaporates into an echo and the reverb doesn't return. Jamie can no longer feel her tongue and her mouth grows until her teeth no longer touch. She takes an exhale that doesn't stop. Yet, an inhale penetrates her torso. Clenching her fist, her fingers tighten past her palms and never stops tightening. The expanse descends.

Touch. Sensation. Form. Skin, shoulder, bones, heart, lips, breath, words, sound, ears, noise, sight, color, mass, dimension, space, place, home, sleep, move, eat, world, sun, stars, morning, night, nature, animals, people, friends, family, life, alive. I'm alive. Jamie thinks. I think. I am and have been.

"Wow...That was...that was a hell of a thing," Jamie mentions to the street. She looks up to the expanding celestial phenomenon known as the Reality Squall. She finds her own hands and relishes the fact they're still there. She touches her face and embraces the ability to smell, taste, speak and hear. "I'm uh...I don't know how or why but...I don't....happy, but...I don't think people are supposed to experience whatever that was."

Jamie rolls to her side, facing the sound of a familiar beeping. Her truck is parked in the middle of the street and the driver's side door is open. "Oh...wow." Jamie rolls to her stomach and slowly gets to her feet. She feels every muscle, appreciating their ache. "Ugh, fuck me, everything hurts," Jamie mentions as she closes the door.

"You're telling me," Anita answers.

"Shit," Jamie says, surprised by her daughter's presence. She's kneeling on the ground, out of breath with a road rash on her cheek and neck. Anita stands and dusts herself off as Jamie takes a moment to collect herself. "Holy hell. Jesus, are you okay?"

Anita nods and rotates the shoulder she landed on. "Yeah, yeah. Nothing that won't heal."

"Did you pull me out of that?" Jamie asks.

"I could go without seeing you dead again."

"And we fell out of my truck?"

"I don't know. I think so," Anita says.

"That was, um, that was...thank you."

Anita looks up at the radiant skies. The celestial bodies cast a shadow enveloped in technicolor. "You know how at funerals, the dead body has its arms folded and its eyes and mouth are shut? And for some reason, their cheeks are rosy?"

Jamie knows where this is going but forsakes the idea of trying to avoid it. "Standard funeral body stuff, yeah."

"Yeah, you didn't look like that."

"What...," Jamie swallows the residual acid flavor in her mouth and then her pride. "What happened?"

"Dad and I found you with one eye open, tongue drooping to one side and Jesus fuck you smelled like stale shit. You might have been like that for days."

"I don't know if I should be hearing this."

Anita sneers at Jamie through her brow. "It was from the actual shit."

"Didn't need to hear that but okay."

"Flopped off the side of the bed with trash on the other side."

Jamie stares off into the middle space and visualizes her own death. The image comes to her, clearly, and with little effort. Shame follows the ease of her projection.

"I...I just didn't...what happened?"

"What do you think happened? You sleep like a tornado, eat like a garbage disposal, and drink like an alcoholic because you're an alcoholic. Your organs said fuck this."

"How old were you?"

"Nine."

"Nine? You were fucking nine? I die in two years?"

"Yeah, mom...yeah."

Jamie forgets the sheer impossibility of this scenario. That brief sentence caused the universe to stop. "You called me "mom."

"Genetically. You're genetically my mother. And that comes with baggage," Kimberly argues.

"I know...and it's unfair," Jamie answers.

"You know what though, I don't even know you. You could be from an alternate timeline or actually thirty crabs in a human suit."

"And that's fair."

"But I just thought, hey, if I can jump around in times and realities and shit, maybe I could meet you, you know? See what you were like. Get to know you as an adult."

"I'm glad you did."

"Pfft, fuck off," Kimberly sighs.

"Seriously."

"This was a disaster."

Jamie shrugs, mines for something insightful and ends on "Eh."

"...really?"

"I mean, out of all the potential disasters....'eh.'"

"How can you say that?"

"Life's gonna be a fucked-up mess whether universes or smashing into each other or not. At least I got to hang out with my daughter for a minute."

"You mean your freeloading bum, hitching her way to nowhere."

"Yeah, but you have an actual personality and expectations."

"Oh wow...sounds like you're breaking up with me." Kimberly starts gently tapping her knuckles. Jamie snickers at the sight. "What the fuck are you laughing at?"

"Sorry, I just saw something that made me smile," Jamie hushes.

"Smile? What about this made you smile?" As Kimberly's anger intensifies, so does her volume. "Because I fail to see the humor in any of this shit—" In the midst of Kimberly's rant the forest erupts in activity. "Holy shit! Back! BACK!" Kimberly blusters. The alpha deer creature growls at Kimberly with two accompanying beasts from his herd.

Emitting a sound that resembles a dog snarl with clicking, the three creatures sprint to Kimberly. Jamie grips onto Kimberly's wrist and yanks her behind her own body. "It's okay! Stop!" The alpha stops in his tracks and sways back in forth, showing his teeth. The three keep their fangs facing Kimberly. "It's okay. She's with me. It's okay."

The alpha's lips roll back over his teeth and diligence returns to his sharp face. He looks to Jamie "She good, thanks though." The alpha looks back at Kimberly. He growls a bit as he slowly retreats to his defense of Jamie. "I'm glad you enjoyed the bread."

The alpha grunts as he turns his back on Jamie, disappearing, with his flock, into the dark of the woods. Jamie turns back to Kimberly. "Deer monsters."

"What the fuck?" Kimberly exclaims at nearly being torn apart.

"Look, I'm sorry for...everything." A silence rolls through that is more unsatisfying than uncomfortable, but lives in the same orbit as uncomfortable. Not sure what else they're waiting for or where else to look, Jamie breaks the silence. "What?"

"What do you mean 'What?'" Kimberly retorts.

"I mean what by my what?"

"I mean, that's it?"

"That's really...yeah, doesn't make it less true."

"I just thought they'd be more."

"Well, what can I say Kimmy? I screwed up in a lot of ways."

"Yeah, you did."

Jamie instantly rolls her eyes and excavates her own psyche. She latches onto the compounding fears she's avoided acknowledging. She readies herself, finding the words to articulate her sadness. As if speaking could trigger a landmine, Jamie treads softly. "I didn't take care of myself and..." Jamie lips quiver, fearing the sting of the admission. "And it turned on me. I thought I could just plow through my issues as long as you were fine, but...you know, I just kept letting it get worse and I told myself that it was fine if you were. But no. When one got bad the others got worse. When I attacked you, that was it. I didn't know what to do after that. Just gave up. So yeah, sorry for everything."

"Ah, I...," Kimberly gives up on a response and merely smiles at her mother.

Jamie presses her palms into her eyes. She circumvents crying but her palms are kissed by impending tears. "But then I think, here we are, now. When else are we going to get an opportunity like this."

"What are you thinking?" Kimberly asks.

"Look, I don't know how much time we have together, but at least we have time together."

Kimberly sighs. "What are you thinking, because I don't know if I can handle Pic-A-Lilli's again."

"The fewer folks, the better for me right now."

"Same."

"Come with me to finish my freight," Jamie says while pointing to her truck.

"What? Why?"

"I don't know. I gave away most of the bread to the deer things but there's still equipment in there that needs to be delivered. Plus, look at all the shit we're going to see."

Kimberly looks to the horizon. The galaxy sets and the light from the cosmos compresses into a shimmering beam that glides through forest. Jamie watches the sliver of incandescence glint across Kimberly.

"Gotta pay for drum lessons," Jamie adds.

Kimberly recognizes the history behind that sentence. "R.E.M. Behavioral Disorder" Kimberly adds abruptly.

"What about it?"

"That's your condition. Attacking people in your sleep."

"I was diagnosed when it got too much for your dad. Thought I had it under control. I crossed the line when it came to you. George I can pummel. "

Kimberly looks back at the cosmos "...will I?"

"I think they're in your cards, but you can avoid them if you play them right."

"Hmm, figures."

"That hitchhiker was your father by the way."

"I know."

"Did you drop that hint?"

"I dropped a few."

"Sorry, it took me a minute to put it together. I had to realize I wasn't losing my mind."

"I don't blame you. I thought the same thing."

"Hey, how are we supposed to not..."

"Can I drive?" Kimberly unexpectedly asks.

With a raised eyebrow, Jamie sways her head side to side and ponders Kimberly's proposal. "Shhhhhhhure. You know what you're doing?"

"It's been a minute, but yeah, as long as you're there to spot-check." In a blend of enthusiasm and maternal terror, Jamie nods "Cool, meet you on the other side."

Jamie walks off to the other side of the truck. She takes the long way, moseying around the trailer. When she gets to the back of her truck, she exhales a breath of relief. Scraps of plastic litter the streets from her bread shipment. Shoving the empty crates inside the trailer, she steps up on the grate and closes the door. She realizes the ease in her step. It's a symptom of an inspired psyche, but Jamie deems it a fluke. On her dismount, she finds her logbook strewn on the ground. She picks it up, dusts it off and places it under her arm.

Standing still, she looks down the open road. The road is clear but the forest encasing it is brimming with life. She sits on the gate of the trailer door. The moon, her moon, is in the sky. There's nothing miraculous about it. It's waning and dim. Looking at it induces a nostalgic ease, like indulging in a long-forgotten hometown staple. Jamie wipes away the suppressed tears from her cheeks.

She hears the driver's side door close and nods. "Okay... okay." Standing up, she rolls her shoulder. The impact of crashing out of alternate times and realities has tightened the already taut joint. "Sheesh...," Jamie feels a click that is followed by a slicing nerve pain. "Oof, okay. Gotta work on that." She makes her way to the passenger's side door. "Glad I'm not driving."

Kimberly is adjusting the seat when Jamie steps in. "Whoa, never sat here."

"Same here," Kimberly chimes as she reaches for the end of the wheel. It's still a tad out of reach. "Can I ask you something? And don't be afraid to say no."

Jamie casually flips her hands "Sure. I mean, afraid's my base emotion, so fire away." Jamie finds her thermos by her feet. She tosses the logbook down next to it.

"What were your nightmares?

"My night terrors? Or R.E.M. behaviors terrors? Doesn't have the same ring to them," Jamie comments as she opens her window.

"Yeah? If you don't mind. Don't want to like trigger them or anything."

"Nah, I think talking about them helps." Jamie pours out the remnants of her thermos through the open window and then flicks her birth control sleeve into the woods. "Sorry, old coffee. Dogs."

REALITY SQUALL | 151

"Really?"

"Yeah, well, mostly their teeth," Jamie remarks as she tosses her empty thermos in the back.

"But we had a dog."

"Bob. The little potato."

"Why'd we get a dog if you were terrified of dogs?"

"That's why we got Bob. On top of being as intimidating as a bean bag chair, he was goofy and laid-back."

"Okay, yeah, but why even get a dog then?"

"You wanted a dog," Jamie comments, closing her window.

"Oh...uh—"

"He was a wonderful dog. Is. He's still alive in my timeline.

"Yeah, he was and is. Love that potato." Anita smirks at the memories and starts the engine. "You ready?

"Yeah, whoop, hold on." Jamie reaches into her jacket pocket and puts Skull McCartney on the dashboard. His accordion is deflating. "One last thing." Jamie pulls down the driver's side visor. She clasps the picture of Kimberly and herself onto the mirror. "Okay, now we're ready."

"Well, shit. Good call."

It sputters into gear, but the truck eventually drives into the endless magnificence of simultaneous realities.

THE SHARDS OF CERAMICS FINISH WOBBLING IN THE SPLATTER of milk and cereal. "Oh...oh..." Jamie says aloud, looking at the breakfast debris on the kitchen floor. Seated on her stool, Jamie stands up with an intent she can't discern. With a mind looking to find motivation behind her agency, she comes to realize, there isn't one. Slowly descending back into her stool, she looks around her room. "Huh." She shifts her body over the kitchen counter, categorizing a series of events that just, always or never have transpired. They're there. Buried like an infantile memory, but they're there. "Huh."

She looks to the floor. One mess finds another and, soon, she catalogues all the filth in her apartment. Mentally, she calculates the order of operations. The cereal, dishes, trash, tile, rug, bedroom. What once seemed insurmountable now looks manageable. "Huh."

Billy, Carl, and Jamie have been seated in the locker room for thirty-eight minutes. The conversation hasn't gone past "Hey." Eye contact is scarce and the three have been quietly and politely shuffling through their day. That is the pace and rhythm of the rest of the world.

Jamie looks at her knuckles. She places them together and there's zero compulsion to inflict self-harm. Bringing the knuckles up, she rests her head on her fists. "So..."

"So." Carl immediately responds, snapping out of his trance.

"Did—"

"Yeah."

"And?"

"Uhuh."

"So did I...," Jamie motions to the stunned Billy.

With tight lips and a craven brow, Billy tells the floor "...yes."

"Oh...sorry," Jamie responds.

"It's...it's okay" Billy mutters with a humble grin that flutters into existence just as easily as it leaves.

The three remain silent. Billy reaches into his pocket and retrieves his billfold. He hands it to Jamie. "And, um, sorry."

"It's also okay." Jamie places her hand over the billfold and closes Billy's hand over it. "You're good. Let me know if you need help getting your rig back." She pats Billy's hands before she stands. "Alright...I guess."

As if returning from a prolonged vacation, the three shamble their way through the workday.

"Hey," Jamie chirps to Carl as she opens her locker.

"Yeah?" Carl answers.

"Mind if I join you for workouts again?"

"...that's never been off the table," Carl answers with nothing but genuine warmth.

TIME PASSES ACCORDINGLY

JAMIE PACKS HER DUFFEL BAG ON THE LOCKER ROOM BENCH.
After hanging up her denim jacket, she reaches down to her pile of laundry. Packing the new mainstays in her travel bag always brings forth a reluctant sigh. Atop her plastic bag of toiletries and towels, she fits in her mittens and sleeping bag. Open on both ends to allow her feet air, she can also zipper the bag closed toward her cool feet. It's a safety protocol in case her mittened hands break free and look to escape. She's awoken a few times in a violent rage, trying to unconsciously navigate her way from her conscious trap. Luckily, the gap between each fit is widening. *Just keep doing it until...forever, I guess.*

"Hey, you look good," Sally mentions to Jamie, rounding the corner.

"I do? I mean, I'm trying," Jamie responds as she closes her locker. She's formally dressed in a black-on-black pants suit and jacket.

"Way better than the last time I told you that."

"Yeah, I know. Thanks for lying."

"Anytime."

"This work? I'm going for an Agent Scully on a Causal Friday kinda thing," Jamie remarks, providing a flourish in the direction of her wardrobe.

"Kidding me? Classy as all get out."

"Sure?"

"Belle of the fourth-grade ball."

"I don't want to bring too much razzle-dazzle tonight. It's their night."

"Well, at least bring this?" Sally offers a manila envelope to Jamie.

Jamie opens the envelope and slides an ELD GPS tracker into her hand.

"Ah, thanks," Jamie meekly says to the exiting Sally.

"Sure thing."

"How's that nephew?"

"The dude loves hemp now," Sally says in the doorway.

"Good job."

"She's going to kill it tonight, Jamie." Before she exits, Sally takes a moment to acknowledge the sincerity.

"Thank you."

***

"You're welcome," Carl answers in the parking lot of the local grade school. Parents in beige formal wear shuttle their way inside the bustling building.

"And your car just smells way better than mine," Jamie adds as she walks in step with Carl.

"The smell you smelled this evening is 'Ocean Storm.'"

"Whoa ho, classy."

"Speaking of classy, this vest, no jacket thing working on me?" Carl asks to his formal attire.

"Hell yeah. And we match."

"It's just, when I added the upper girth, shit looks boxy."

"My heart bleeds," Jamie says as the two enter the school hallways through massive double doors. Recital posters are draped along the walls as teachers sell minuscule refreshments and older siblings brood in corners.

"I'm hitting the bathroom. Meet you in there," Carl says, walking off.

"Sure thing." Jamie walks through the school with the distant sound of drumming echoing throughout the halls. George is on his cell phone, standing outside of the auditorium doors. He's wearing a brown corduroy suit with a white button down underneath. Carl walks past him and the contrast between the two causes Jamie to giggle.

"Hey, George."

"Jamie, hey. I got to go, yeah, you, too." George hangs up his phone.

"How's she doing?"

"Ready. Very very ready. My eardrums are sure."

"Awesome. You? You good?" Jamie asks.

"Meh, not bad. All is not bad," George answers with a nonthreatening sheen.

"Bob?"

"Swabbed. You still good to pick them up this weekend?

"Of course."

"And the summer? Still on track?"

"...very," Jamie responds in a hush.

"Not sure how I'm going to feel with a week of uninterrupted sleep."

"It's good, believe me," Jamie scoffs.

"Alright, looking forward to it. Your mom's already in there. She saved you and Carl a seat."

"Wow, okay. Cool. Guess everything's...fine?" Jamie cannot recall ever saying or believing that. It felt unfair to say so effortlessly, let alone so sincerely.

"I'll see you in there. You want anything?" George asks as he walks off toward the folding table concession stand.

"I'm good, thanks." Jamie rolls her shoulders with relative ease. She enters the auditorium. As parents and teachers wander in, Jamie looks to the show curtains. She can't help but smile from a sound that almost wasn't, in a life that almost ended. The orchestra rehearsal bleeds through the fabric and the drums absolutely dominate.

THE END

A NOTE ON THE TYPE

The text of this book is set in Minion 3, an updated and expanded version of Robert Slimbach's iconic text typeface. The first version of Minion was released in 1990 and is inspired by classical, old style typefaces of the late Renaissance, a period of elegant, beautiful, and highly readable type designs. Minion Pro combines the aesthetic and functional qualities that make text type highly readable with the versatility of Open-Type digital technology, yielding unprecedented flexibility and typographic control, whether for lengthy text or display settings.

Robert Slimbach, who joined Adobe in 1987, began working seriously on type and calligraphy four years earlier in the type drawing department of Autologic in Newbury Park, California. Since then, he has concentrated primarily on designing text faces for digital technology, drawing inspiration from classical sources. In 1991, he received the Prix Charles Peignot from Association Typographique Internationale for excellence in type design. Slimbach now directs Adobe's type design program.

The heading of this book are set in Chinese Rocks Regular, designed by Raymond Larabie. Typodermic Fonts—a friendly and down-to-earth type foundry—was started in 2001 by Larabie, a super creative Canadian designer who loves exploring the world of typography. Working from his cozy studio in Nagoya, Japan, Ray has been putting together a fantastic collection of fonts that designers across the globe have come to appreciate.

The title of this book is set in Cherie Bomb, by Great Scott!, an independent type foundry based in Stockholm, Sweden.

Composed by Clever Crow Consulting and Design
Pittsburgh, Pennsylvania

ACKNOWLEDGMENTS

Originally, I wanted to write a spooky long-dark-highway story you could read in any order—an existential tribute to that hypnotically eerie feeling of driving alone at night. I love it. Like looking down a shadowy flight of steps but at seventy miles per hour. Wasn't my face red when I realized I was actually writing about my mother? Something I also love, but in a totally different and emotionally complex manner.

My mother's an addict. She has treated her body with complete neglect and has fed her brain's unhealthy impulses for decades. It was hard to watch, let alone live with, someone who only knew want. It was the worst day of our lives when my father died in 2023. She leaned on him for support as her health severely waned. I did and am doing my best to see to her comfort, but it's not enough. It'll never be enough. Deteriorated from a lifetime of unregulated compulsions, there's little hope left in her broken body.

It's crushing to wittiness. I have a lot of feelings about my mother, and they're all as intense and harrowing as a son can feel about a parent. I've felt guilty for not being able to provide the emotional support she needs, but I'm afraid there isn't a floor to that trench. So, if there's anything to glean from this book or, at the very least, this acknowledgment, take care of yourself. People want to see you love yourself. I don't know who you are reading this sentence, but I can tell you without a shred of a doubt that I am rooting for you. And I can guarantee you, I'm not the only one.

ABOUT THE AUTHOR

After finding high school physics exceedingly difficult, Jason Krawczyk decided to pursue his original passion for filmmaking. After university, he started "Alternate Ending Studios." A production company that has shot and produced numerous music videos, commercials, and shorts, but left maintained the goal of producing feature films. Jason has written and directed AES' first feature-length project *The Briefcase.* In 2015 Jason wrote and directed the Henry Rollins horror-comedy *He Never Died,* which premiered at South By Southwest and is currently streaming on Netflix. A sequel, *She Never Died* was released in 2020, with a separate project *Sunset Superman* filming in 2022.

Jason plans to evolve his craft for storytelling and writing in the cinematic and literary landscape until his foreseeable demise.

YOU MAY ALSO LIKE:

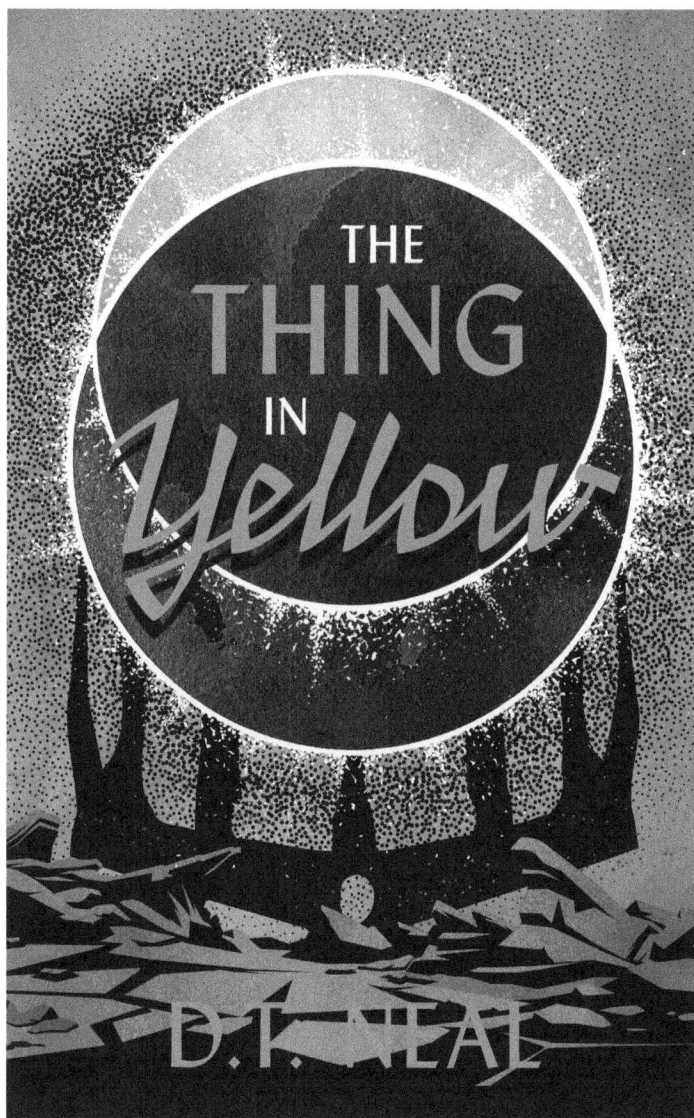

THE
THING
IN
Yellow

D. T. NEAL

"THE KING WOULD BE PROUD...
GREAT COLLECTION OF CREEPY, UNSETTLED STORIES.
WELL WRITTEN, BLEAK, CRUEL AND UNKIND STORIES."
—MR. E. C. YOUNG, AMAZON REVIEW

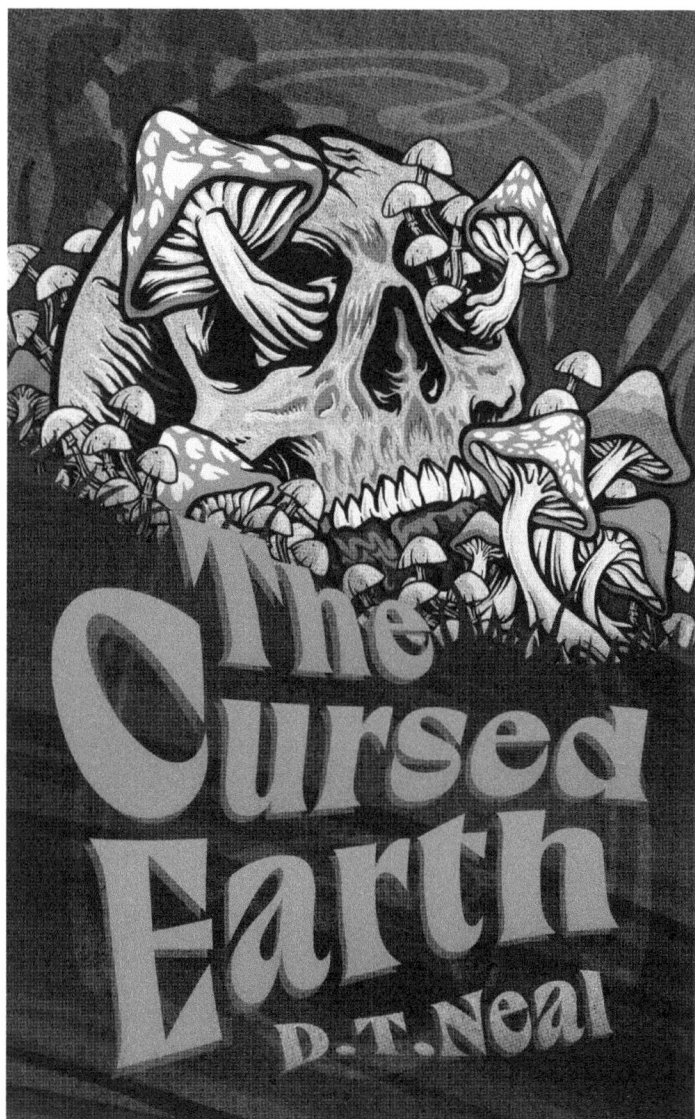

The Cursed Earth

D. T. Neal

"THIS BOOK IS AMAZING...
IMMERSIVE, ENGAGING, AND FUN.
I WOULD DEFINITELY PUT THIS BOOK AS ONE OF THE BEST
BOOKS I HAVE READ IN 2022."
—TASHA, GOODREADS REVIEW

N*P

NOSETOUCH PRESS ™

Nosetouch Press is an independent book publisher tandemly based in Chicago and Pittsburgh. We are dedicated to bringing some of today's most energizing fiction to readers around the world.

Our commitment to classic book design in a digital environment brings an innovative and authentic approach to the traditions of literary excellence.

*We're Out There™
NOSETOUCHPRESS.COM
Horror | Science Fiction | Fantasy | Mystery
Supernatural | Gothic | Weird

Printed in the USA
CPSIA information can be obtained
at www.ICGtesting.com
JSHW020041300724
67251JS00004B/22